HIDDEN PATH

A BODHI KING NOVEL

MELISSA F. MILLER

BROWN STREET BOOKS

Published by Brown Street Books.

Brown Street Books ISBN: 978-1-940759-34-0

ALSO BY MELISSA F. MILLER

The Sasha McCandless Legal Thriller Series

Irreparable Harm

Inadvertent Disclosure

Irretrievably Broken

Indispensable Party

Lovers and Madmen (Novella)

Improper Influence

A Marriage of True Minds (Novella)

Irrevocable Trust

Irrefutable Evidence

A Mingled Yarn (Novella)

Informed Consent

International Incident

Imminent Peril

The Humble Salve (Novella)

The Aroostine Higgins Novels

Critical Vulnerability

Chilling Effect

Calculated Risk

The Bodhi King Novels

Dark Path

Lonely Path

Hidden Path

The We Sisters Three Romantic Comedic Mysteries

Rosemary's Gravy

Sage of Innocence

Thyme to Live

Lost and Gowned

What we must understand is that the industries, processes, and inventions created by modern science can be used either to subjugate or liberate. The choice is up to us.

HENRY A. WALLACE

Food is a weapon.

EARL BUTZ

Bija Niyama, order of germs or seeds (physical organic order) [is one of the five natural orders];

e.g., rice produced from rice-seed, sugary taste from sugar cane or honey etc.

"BUDDHISM IN A NUTSHELL,"
NARADA MAHATHERA, ACCESS TO
INSIGHT (BCBS EDITION), 30
NOVEMBER 2013

CHAPTER ONE

Onatah, Illinois
Just before midnight, Sunday night

Zhang San slipped through the garden on silent feet. Guided only by the moon and the faint glow of lights from the distant highway, he crept confidently along the path leading to the meditation labyrinth.

He reached the maze and skirted its left edge. Then he continued into the tall grass of the meadow buffering the property from the narrow road. He emerged from the grass and swung his head around. He dropped down into the drainage ditch and landed in a crouch.

When he straightened to standing, his mouth was dry. This brief period of visibility from the road was the most nerve-wracking part of the trip. He broke into a run.

Just two tenths of a kilometer, he reminded himself. A mere minute—slightly less, actually. At his pace, he generally covered the distance in just over fifty-five seconds.

He flew over the uneven ground until the road curved to the right. He kept running, no longer exposed to any cars that might happen by at this hour. He stopped when he reached the corner of a metal cattle fence.

He counted in three posts from the end, crouched directly to the right of the third post, and felt around on the ground for the top of the hollow metal spike. A cloud that had been covering the moon graciously moved, providing more light. He spotted the spike's head, just slightly protruding from the dirt, and yanked it out of the damp earth.

He pried the cap off and turned the spike upside down over his palm. A folded slip of paper fluttered into his hand. He pocketed the scrap and placed a wadded-up tissue inside the spike.

As he recapped the spike, he scanned the empty fields around him. He'd yet to encounter another living soul on one of his dead drop runs, but complacency was an agent's worst enemy. Especially in a place like this—all wide open spaces and windswept fields. There were no choke points at which to shake a tail—or at least make him for what he was. San felt as though the prairie itself had eyes and was watching him.

He was ready for this assignment to be over. He longed for congested urban streets, elbow-to-elbow pedestrians jostling for place, as cars, trucks, and buses sped by in the streets. He missed the noise.

He returned the spike to the dirt and used the heel of his shoe to drive it into the ground. He took a deep breath and filled his lungs with the cool night air. Then he turned back the way he'd come and ran.

From his post in the old barn, Gavriil trained his binoculars on the Chinese man and watched his quick, economical movements. San was fast. He held the dead drop spike in his hand for less than twenty seconds before it was back in the dirt and he was sprinting away.

Gavriil pushed himself up from the floor and brushed the hay from the elbows of his sweater. Now, he had a decision to make: Did he intercept San and take the paper from his right front pocket; remove the item

San had deposited in the spike; or wait to see who came to get it—getting a bead on San's contact?

Back when he'd worked for the agency, it would have been a no-brainer. Identify San's contact. Anyone San had turned was already vulnerable and could be a wealth of information—or, even more valuable, a prospective double agent.

But, Gavriil reminded himself, he *didn't* work for the agency anymore. And he hadn't been hired to turn a Chinese spy. He also hadn't been hired to tail San, although doing so made his work easier. But he knew where to find San. He could keep his paper—for now.

Decision made, he crept out of the barn and stepped in among the tall rows of corn. The soft swish of cornstalks giving way as he brushed past them was covered by the whisper of the wind. Like a shadow, he wound his way through the corn.

When he reached the last row, he cut a fast diagonal line to the fenced-in pasture. At the third post from the left, he dug the spike out of the ground. Still crouching, he uncapped it and removed a tissue that had been folded into a small, thick square, as if an elementary school kid had lost a tooth at lunchtime and was keeping it safe inside until he could slip it under his pillow.

He unfolded the tissue to reveal a smooth item roughly the size and shape of a baby tooth. But this was no pearly white. It was a single, pale yellow seed. Gavriil allowed himself a small smile before he removed a tiny plastic bag, the type that held extra buttons for a jacket, from his pocket.

He shook a darker yellow seed out of the bag and dropped the one from the spike into it. After carefully resealing the bag, he returned it to his pocket. Then he wrapped his replacement seed in San's tissue, stuffed it into the spike, and jabbed the spike into the ground.

Only then did he return to standing. He cracked his back, stiff from the hours of surveillance, then rolled his neck.

He jammed his hands into his pockets and walked along the berm of the road, the binoculars bouncing on the strap hung around his neck. He strolled at a casual pace, just an owl lover, out for his nightly nocturnal walkabout, hoping to catch a glimpse of a great horned owl, a barn owl, or maybe, if he was very lucky, a snowy white.

CHAPTER TWO

Chicago, Illinois
Monday afternoon

Bodhi King closed his eyes for just a moment after he settled in the back of the cab. He'd left the hotel in Quebec City well before dawn to make the day's first flight to Toronto, only to encounter a delay on the second leg.

After a long, unexplained wait, the prop plane took off for Chicago nearly two hours late. He'd been traveling for ten hours by this point and yearned for a still, quiet moment.

The driver had other plans. "You in town for business or pleasure?"

He opened his eyes. "Just passing through. I'm meeting a friend for lunch then heading to Onatah."

In the rearview mirror, he could see the cab driver furrow his forehead. "Onatah, huh? Never heard of it. What's there?"

"Mainly cornfields," Bodhi told him, unsurprised that a Chicagoan had no familiarity with the postage-stamp town just about ninety minutes due south. "But there's also a monastery. I'm going for a retreat."

"A retreat. You a monk?"

"No."

He wasn't a monk. Just someone in need of seven days of silence to clear his mind, reset his course, and work through an issue that had arisen out of nowhere.

After more than a decade of celibacy and solitude, he'd just spent a week in the company of the only woman he'd ever loved. To say the encounter had knocked him off-balance didn't begin to do justice to the unmoored feeling in his center.

A week spent in contemplative quiet at The Prairie Buddhist Center would put him back on his path. Or, at least, it would point him in the right direction.

"Huh." A brief silence. Then, "How 'bout those Bears?"

It took him a moment to realize the man was talking football, not asking him his thoughts on the animal.

He flashed a wry smile. "Sorry, pal. I'm a Steelers fan."

"Bah." The cab driver lifted a hand and batted the thought out of the air. For the rest of the drive, he delivered a running monologue on the comparative greatness of the Steel Curtain Defense of the 1970s versus the Bears' famed 46 Defense of 1985.

Bodhi settled back against the seat, stopped listening, and let the words rush over him like water.

Nolan was waiting for him in front of the Thai restaurant when the cab driver pulled over, still waxing poetic about Buddy Ryan's defensive genius. Bodhi paid the fare, shouldered his bag, and exited the back seat.

Nolan greeted him with an enthusiastic handshake and a slap on the back.

"Long time, no see, man. How's it going?"

"Great. You could've waited inside."

Nolan waved his hand. "Nah. I'll be inside for eighteen hours today."

As the Chief of the Emergency Medicine Department of a busy urban hospital, Nolan McDermott worked an unforgiving schedule. But Bodhi had never seen the man without a grin on his still-boyish, freckled face.

"Does this place have patio seating? Or we could get it to go—eat in a park somewhere?" Bodhi offered.

"No worries. I'll walk to the hospital after lunch. I'll get my allotment of Vitamin D and fresh air on the way." He pulled the door open and ushered Bodhi inside.

The restaurant was spa-like with simple furnishing, bamboo, and natural fabrics. Nolan greeted the waiter like an old friend and ordered water and jasmine tea for the table.

"Do you mind leaving ourselves in Chef Aran's hands? He's a magician with vegan food."

Bodhi blinked. "Sure. But since when are you a vegan?"

"Since I hit the big 4-0 and cheeseburgers started collecting at my waistline." He laughed then turned to the waiter, "Please tell Aran to wow my vegan friend."

The waiter bowed his head and smiled. As he turned to leave, he said to Bodhi, "You're in for a treat."

Nolan leaned back and arranged his long legs under the table. "So, what were you doing in Canada anyway?"

He was one of a handful of friends who Bodhi considered like brothers—and, in one case, a sister. Bodhi and Nolan weren't particularly diligent about staying in contact, but they could seamlessly pick back up as if there'd been no lapse—no matter how many years had gone by without their having spoken. In this case, it had been eight—the last time he'd seen Nolan was on his wedding day. He made a mental note to ask how Katie was doing.

"I was on a panel at the North American Forensic Pathology Symposium."

"Sweet. That's a nice get."

"Eliza Rollins was on the panel, too."

Nolan's red eyebrows shot up and met at his hairline. "Eliza, whoa ... have you seen her since med school?"

"No. And, if you remember, we weren't exactly on good terms when we graduated."

He nodded slowly. "That's right. You broke up with her to focus on your residency."

It was an oversimplification, but Bodhi resisted the urge to defend his younger self's actions. "Basically."

Nolan sucked in his breath. "Awkward. How's she doing?"

"It *was* awkward, at first; but we ended up spending a lot of time together."

"Oh, really?" His grin spoke volumes.

"Not like that. Eliza's doing great. She's the parish coroner in some small town in Louisiana. And she's dating the local chief of police. It sounded like they were pretty serious. We didn't really talk about it—we were too busy figuring out what happened to a woman who'd been declared dead but we found wandering along a country road."

The waiter returned with two glasses of water, a small teapot, and a set of mugs. He placed the drinkware and teapot on the table and asked if there was anything else they needed.

"We're all set," Nolan assured him.

Bodhi poured the tea while Nolan mused under his breath.

"Declared dead woman hanging out on the side of the road." He lifted his head and twisted his mouth to the side. "What kind of symposium was this, exactly?"

"It was a standard medical conference. The interesting stuff was all extracurricular. Well, except for one of our co-panelists trying to have us killed. Look, it's a long story—"

"You don't say," Nolan deadpanned.

Bodhi nearly spit his tea on the tablecloth when he burst into laughter. After he caught his breath, he summarized the highlights for Nolan.

"There's a designer drug—at least in Canada, it's called Solo. You should be on the lookout for it in your ER because it's nasty. The developer's in custody and working with the authorities on an antidote, but you know how it goes. Some other enterprising dealer is no doubt trying to reverse engineer the formula as we sit here. I hope it doesn't cross the border."

Nolan nodded sadly. "Me, too. We've got enough to deal with here without a hot new killer drug. What is it?"

"A combination of neurotoxins that apparently caused an animating, invigorating high. But can cause central nervous system and respiratory paralysis and, eventually, the arrest of brain function."

Nolan grimaced. "Not a nice way to go."

"Or not go. Some of the overdoses didn't actually die. They were more or less zombified. Anyway, Eliza and I worked together to help the victims and find the black market chemist."

"And then she went back home to her hunky police chief and you realized you're approaching middle age all alone?"

Bodhi sipped his tea. "Something like that."

"Which brings you to Chicago, why?"

"I'm on my way to the Prairie Buddhist Center for a week-long silent retreat. I figure it'll do me good to have some quiet contemplative time."

"Where's this center?"

"A town in central Illinois called Onatah."

Nolan snorted. "It should be plenty quiet down there. Nothing but cornfields and ... cornfields."

"It sounds perfect."

"So, really, no talking for a week? What will you do?"

They paused as steaming dishes of fragrant curries and bowls of soup arrived at the table. After the food had been served, he tried to explain the allure of a silent retreat to a man who thrived on the cacophony of the emergency room at work and the more joyous racket of a five-year old and three-year old at home.

"The Prairie Center is sort of unusual. Here in the U.S., many of the retreat centers are secular. Of those that aren't, most are Mayahana, or Zen focused. A handful practice Theravada Buddhism. Even fewer are esoteric or tantric. But The Prairie Center is explicitly *not* secular and isn't tied to a specific school or sect of Buddhism."

"So it's the equivalent of a nondenominational or nonsectarian church?"

"Right. So, at Prairie, retreats are an opportunity for practitioners to expand their knowledge of other practices. That means there are lectures, meditations, and readings based on the various sects and schools, in addition to the usual mindful eating and working sessions, noble silences, and seated and walking meditations."

"Sounds boring."

Bodhi shrugged. "I could use some boredom."

He lifted a spoonful of soup to his mouth. An explosion of ginger, lemongrass, and chilies burst onto his taste buds. Nolan watched his face.

"Pretty amazing, isn't it?"

"It really is."

Nolan laughed. "Told you."

They ate in silence for a few moments. Then Bodhi rested his spoon on the side of his saucer. "How are Katie and the kids?"

"They're great, man. Katie's planning to join a pediatric practice in our neighborhood next year when the little one starts pre-K. It's a wild ride with Noah and Serena; I won't pretend it's not. But they're fun, you know? Exhausting, but fun."

Bodhi nodded. A week ago, Nolan's idea of fun would have struck him as a messy attachment. But now? Well, now he didn't know. That's why he was headed to Onatah. To figure it out in a place of peace.

CHAPTER THREE

Onatah, Illinois
Monday, suppertime

C hief of Police Bette Clark stifled a sigh and raked her fingers through her long white hair. She wasn't old enough to have white hair, she thought for what had to be the eight thousandth time. It was her oft-repeated silent lament.

Her job had drained the color right out of her hair. But it would hardly do for Onatah's head law enforcement officer to be seen in Shelia's Shear Beauty Salon, sitting under a bubble dryer with dye on her head. It was undignified. So, she rocked her white locks with authority but secretly planned to dye them mermaid blue the day she retired. Or maybe a shocking pink.

Regardless, the mess she was dealing with right now

was Exhibit A in the collection of evidence that her job was prematurely aging her.

On the other side of her battered metal desk, Jason Durbin, red-faced and blustering, was struggling mightily to keep hold of his temper. Judging from the way the veins bulged out on his tanned forearms, he was losing the battle.

A few feet away from him—just out of reach of Jason's meaty fists—Mark Olson was sneering. Whether the sneer was directed at her or Jason, Bette couldn't tell, but regardless of the target, it was pissing them both off. She allowed herself a brief fantasy of wiping the expression off Olson's face with a right hook of her own.

Then, she pushed herself to standing and threw back her shoulders. She reflexively rested her right hand on the butt of the gun at her hip. A wordless reminder as to who was in charge around here.

"Now, that's enough, you two." She waited until the glaring men looked away from one another and met her eyes before continuing. "Jason, I know you know that Supra Seed has a commission especially to address the issue of crop death from pesticide drift. If you've got a problem with Mark's spraying practices, that's the venue to—"

"And you and I also both know Mark's been warned before about using Crop-Clear when the winds are up.

Supra Seed's just gonna slap him on the wrist again. Meanwhile, I've got a field full of withering corn, chief. That's a lost harvest." Jason was just about shaking with fury.

Mark shrugged, unconcerned. "Take it up with the commission, Jason. Like she said, there's a process in place. They'll compensate you for your lost crop, if you can substantiate your damages. Or you could go to the state about it. Now, if we're done here, Donna's holding my dinner."

Bette narrowed her eyes. The crack about complaining to the state was just an effort to get under Jason's skin. The state regulatory board had a backlog that stretched into the last millennium, which was the whole reason Supra Seed set up a private board in the first place.

"You go on home, Mark. Give Donna my best. But I don't want any more calls from you or her about Jason trespassing. Hear?"

"Talk to him."

"I'm talking to you. If you see him near your land, go on out and offer him a cup of coffee, don't call in a complaint. You're neighbors for Pete's sake."

Mark appeared to be chewing on the inside of his cheek in an effort to bite back his words. The effort failed. "You're right, Chief Clark. We're neighbors. So, let me give you some neighborly advice, Jason. Stop being a stubborn hippie. Sign up for Supra Seed's grower program, already. You'll increase your crop yield; your quality will be more even; and you can buy their crop management software and automate your growing. Embrace progress; embrace technology."

Bette massaged her forehead. Why would Mark give an organic farmer the Supra Seed hard sell? Was he *trying* to get Jason arrested?

As if on cue, Jason lunged at him, shrieking, "Poison! You're poisoning the earth and your children with that crap! What do you think is in your precious seeds? How do you think they can be immune to that blasted pesticide—do you think it's magic?"

Bette raced around to the front of the desk and shoved herself between the two men. Jason bumped up against her, trying to get at Mark, and she grabbed his forearms.

"No, Jason. I think it's *science.*" Mark laughed.

"Get out of here." She forced the words out from between clenched teeth. "Now, Mark."

Mark Olson tipped his ball cap at her before striding out of her office. "Good night, chief. Jason."

She waited until she heard his pickup sputter to life out front. Then she released Jason from her grip.

He lowered his eyes to the floor and mumbled, "Sorry, chief."

She exhaled a long, exasperated breath. "Go on home. Call the Supra Seed commission in the morning, okay?"

His face was dark, and she could tell he was fighting back tears. "For all the good it'll do."

"It won't do any good if you don't call them." She paused. "You have any of those free-range eggs to sell?"

He wouldn't meet her eyes. "I don't want your charity, Bette."

"That's Chief Clark to you. And it's not charity, Jason. I need to eat, for crying out loud. Now, do you have eggs or am I gonna have to go to Bag-n-Buy?"

"I've got eggs."

"Good. I'll stop by the stand tomorrow. Now, Jason, you've gotta get a handle on your temper."

"Yes, chief," he said in a subdued tone.

He sounded for all the world like a chastened schoolboy, which, frankly, seemed fitting since she felt for all the world like a middle school teacher.

"Good night."

He nodded and shuffled out of her office.

She eyed the clock and started to fantasize about her nightly vodka tonic. It was her one vice—a parting gift from her predecessor. Chief Williams had told her in his somber baritone at his retirement party, "Bette, pick yourself a signature cocktail. Make a date with one every night after work. But only one. You never know when that phone's gonna ring, after all."

At the time, she'd smiled indulgently. But in the five years she'd been chief, that promise of that nightly drink had become a lifeline. One large ice cube, the best tonic water Bag-n-Buy sold, and two fingers of vodka consumed in complete silence while she sat on her back deck, no matter the weather.

Just forty-five more minutes. Then she could lock the door to her office and put her warring farmers out of her mind until morning—or until one of them shot the other one, whichever came first.

CHAPTER FOUR

The low-cost bus from Chicago to Terre Haute, Indiana, stopped in a handful of small towns on its roughly two-hundred mile journey. Onatah wasn't one of them. But the bus driver had assured Bodhi Onatah was just a flat, ten-mile walk from the town of Elm, which was on the route.

So when the bus wheezed and rattled to a stop at the Traveler's Haven in Elm, he followed the crowd down the steps and into the parking lot. They headed for the restrooms and donut counter, and he stood near the edge of the lot and oriented himself.

The bus driver walked over, his unlit cigarette dangling from his mouth. "You want that two-lane road there. It'll wind through a bunch of cornfields. You just stay on it, and it'll take you to the heart of Onatah. If you're lucky, someone will pick you up. Folks still do that around here." He gestured at a thin ribbon of highway that intersected with the interstate.

"Thanks." Bodhi stuck out his hand.

The driver blinked down at it and then gave it a cautious shake. Bodhi slung his bag over his shoulders and tightened the straps. He crossed the weedy patch that separated the parking lot from the interstate highway and waited for an opening in the flow of traffic. Then he hustled across to the cloverleaf and hiked down a grassy slope until he reached the road to Onatah.

He squinted up at the hazy sky. The sun was low, ready to set. He checked his watch. He'd have to hurry if he didn't want to travel most of the way to town in total darkness. He started walking.

As promised, the road was flat. The scenery consisted almost entirely of tall cornfields on both sides of the asphalt. The occasional red barn or old farmhouse appeared back behind the fields. He encountered four trucks and one car; two deer; and a flock of migrating geese. And loads of hand-lettered signs stuck into the shoulder of the road. They read 'Vote No on GMO'; 'Preserve Onatah's Family Farms'; 'Home of a Proud Supra Seed Farmer'; 'Hybrid Seeds = Better Yields, Lower Prices, Higher Profits'; and variations of those two apparently contrary sentiments.

As the sun sank lower behind the small hills, a chill

settled on the air. He jammed his hands deeper into his jacket pockets and quickened his pace. The tall steeple of a church was visible in the distance. He recalled Onatah's layout from the online map he and Nolan had pulled up at the restaurant. The Lutheran church was situated on the town square right across from the feed store. The Prairie Center was just a half mile beyond the square. He was nearly there.

A moment later, the purr of a car engine sounded behind him. He turned and saw a gleaming white sedan edging to the shoulder and slowing to a crawl. The driver was a woman, alone. She buzzed down the passenger window as the car came even with him.

"Do you want a ride to town?" she called.

He hesitated. Rural Illinois or not, it wasn't safe for a single woman to be picking up hitchhikers. But his feet were numb from cold.

"Are you sure that's a good idea?"

She eyed him. "You look harmless enough. But just in case you're a serial killer, you should know I'm a third degree black belt in kung fu. So if you try anything, I'll have to break your arms. Maybe a leg, too."

His laugh came from deep within his chest. "Fair enough."

He stepped over to the car and she unlocked the passenger side door. He hurried inside and blew on his hands to warm them. He looked over at her as she pulled back into the travel lane and brought the car up to cruising speed.

"Thanks for the lift. I'm Bodhi King, and I'm not a serial killer."

She smiled. "You're welcome, Bodhi King. I'm Hannah Lee Lin. And I really am a black belt."

He believed her. Even seated behind the wheel of the car, she carried herself with an unmistakable air of strength and poise. She sat completely erect, hands light on the steering wheel, eyes alert and unblinking.

After a silence, she said, "Where are you headed, anyway? There's not much in Onatah."

"I'm going to the Buddhist retreat center outside town."

"The Prairie Center? I suppose I ought to have guessed—with a name like Bodhi." She cut her eyes toward him and gave him an appraising look. "Zen or Theravada?"

He felt his jaw hinge open. "Uh, a little bit of both, but I'm most familiar with Theravada practice. Are you ... Buddhist?" He asked the question hesitantly. It was one thing for her to make assumptions based on his name, but he didn't want her to think that he was stereotyping her because she was Asian.

She took no offense, though. "Oh, no. Not me. I'm

not religious. I'm a scientist," she said as if that explained her beliefs—or lack thereof.

"Oh? So am I."

She pursed her lips and studied him. "Really? What kind of scientist are you?"

"I'm a forensic pathologist."

"Ah, you're a medical doctor. It makes sense that you'd be a person of faith—you deal in life and death, after all."

"Well, I don't treat patients—not living ones, anyway. I feel more like a scientist than a doctor."

She considered his answer. "I can see that. I'm a plant pathologist."

"I beg your pardon?"

"It's really a thing," she assured him with a giggle. "I work with plant geneticists to create disease-resistant corn."

"Corn?" he echoed.

"Right. My specialty is in phenotyping maize hybrids. Which is how a Chinese-American girl from San Francisco ended up in Onatah, Illinois—where the closest thing to decent Sichuan food is the rice curries at The Prairie Center's community potlucks. I'll give you a ride to the center."

"Are you sure?"

"Sure. It's on my way home. I rent the second floor

of an old farmhouse just about a quarter mile down the road from there."

"Maybe you can stop in and see if there's any curry left from dinner."

"That's tempting, but I've got an early morning tomorrow."

"Seed emergency?"

"You laugh, but yes. There's a big storm brewing."

"Why?"

She slowed the car and turned to look at him. "Did you notice all the signs along the roadside?"

"Sure. Half of them are railing against GMOs and the other half are extolling the virtues of Supra Seed, whatever that is."

"Supra Seed is the company I work for. We've developed Maize46, a disease-resistant corn seed that could help feed a lot of starving people while allowing farmers to be more efficient about their use of water and resources. It's a big leap toward a sustainable global corn crop."

"But?"

She sighed. "Yes, there's always a *but*. But, the pesticide that the company developed to support the product is prone to drift."

"What does that mean?"

"A farmer who plants Maize46 gets crop management software and Crop-Clear along with the seeds. Sensors positioned in the field send information to the software, which analyzes how the corn is growing. The software program lets the farmer know when and how much to water and when to spray Crop-Clear."

"Sounds very precise."

She let out a frustrated breath, and her long bangs danced over her forehead. "It is. But it doesn't take into account the wind—although I'm told the engineers are working on that. That's a big oversight. Maize46 is bred to resist Crop-Clear. The farmer can overspray the entire field without worrying if it gets on the corn. But, if there's a breeze and it drifts into a neighboring field that's *not* growing Maize46 ..."

"It harms the neighbor's crop," he finished for her.

"It does more than harm it. It annihilates it." Her expression was grim. "Our farmers are cautioned not to spray when it's windy, but they're human. They have their own investment to worry about. So, sometimes they spray anyway."

They fell silent again as they passed through the center of town. Only a handful of buildings were lit. Most of the commercial center was dark and quiet.

"Human nature being what it is, maybe your biochemists should work on a formulation that sticks to the plants better—one that's less prone to drifting."

Bodhi had to imagine the seed company had thought of that already, but it seemed that if they had it would be easy enough to implement.

Hannah snorted. "That would solve our problem but it would mean an uptick in business for you. One of our competitors did exactly that to make *their* pesticide stickier. And they're being sued because it looks as if the combination of the pesticide and the chemical to make it adhere better may *also* cause it to adhere to human cells and damage them."

"Cancer?"

"Cancer."

"Oh." She was right. They were in a bad spot.

When she spoke again, her voice was troubled. "It's turned ugly. It's getting near the end of harvest time now, so the farmers are starting to tally their damages for the year. And it's getting heated in town. This is a black eye we really want to avoid. So there's an all-hands-on deck meeting tomorrow at seven a.m."

She turned off the road and bumped up the long driveway to The Prairie Center's main house.

As she came to a stop near the house, he said, "Are you sure you don't want to come inside? You have to eat, after all."

She smiled wanly. "Maybe some other time. It was nice to meet you, Dr. King."

"It was nice to meet you, too. Thanks for the lift and for not breaking my arms."

As he climbed out of the car, she leaned over and called to him. "Bodhi? Please don't say anything to anybody about ... what I told you. I'm probably talking out of turn."

He turned. "Then you're in luck. Tomorrow morning, I start a seven-day silent retreat. My lips are sealed. Kind of literally. But don't worry, I wouldn't mention it anyway."

She gave him a level look. "No, you wouldn't, would you? Thank you." She raised the window and executed a tight three-point turn, spinning up gravel under her tires.

Bodhi stood on the porch and watched until the car's tail lights shrank down to pinpoints and then, finally, disappeared into the night.

CHAPTER FIVE

Tuesday

5:00 A.M.

The singing bowl rang out one resonant note and vibrated in the dark pre-dawn house. Someone had struck the large, metal standing bell with a wooden stick. It was time to wake up.

Bodhi rose and padded to the shared bathroom at the end of the hall to wash his face and brush his teeth. The air was cool and hushed, as if even the house itself intended to be silent for a week.

He returned to the dormitory room and dressed quietly, so as not to wake his three roommates—only one of whom stirred at the sound of the bell. The bell would ring again, more insistently, in fifteen minutes.

He walked soundlessly down the old wooden stairs

to the parlor, where he checked the whiteboard displaying the day's schedule. Sitting meditation would begin at six o'clock, followed by breakfast, and a Dharma talk.

He wandered into the kitchen. The co-leaders of the week's session were making a large vat of oatmeal. Roshi Matsuo, the Zen teacher, diced apples while Bhikkhu Sanjeev, the Theravada monk, grated ginger to add to the oats. They both paused in their work and raised their heads in greeting.

Bodhi bowed his head. "May I help?"

The noble silence wouldn't officially start until the six o'clock meditation session, so he wasn't breaking any rules by speaking. He also knew from past experience that, although the guests were asked not to speak unless they were receiving counseling about their meditation work, the monks and teachers did speak, as needed. While he was a guest, he was also a friend to both Matsuo and Sanjeev. He didn't think they'd take offense at his offer.

And they didn't. Matsuo smiled his wide, slow-blooming smile. It transformed his face. "Yes, please chop the walnuts."

Sanjeev nodded and made space for him at the long butcher block counter.

Bodhi washed his hands at the sink and dried them,

then took his spot. He shook a pile of nuts onto the counter and began to methodically chop them. The knife in his hand settled into a rhythm.

Freed from the obligation of making small talk, he focused on each slice into the meat of the nut. He was mindful of the tree that had borne the walnuts. The sunlight and the rainwater that had nourished the nuts. The farmer who had harvested them. The community that would gather to eat them.

The silence was shattered when the kitchen door slammed open. Feng, a young Theravada monk, rushed through the door. His shaven head was red—Bodhi imagined from the cold—and he huffed out a breath.

"One of the guests is missing," he announced without preamble.

Sanjeev raised his eyebrows. "Did you think you'd find them in the garden?"

Feng bobbed his head. His white apron was bundled together at his waist. He rolled the fabric down and release several small potatoes and three large carrots into a metal colander that stood near the sink.

"No, *bhante*."

"Did you see someone running away?" Matsuo inquired in a mild tone.

Feng shook his head. "No, sir. But the man from New Hampshire did come out onto the porch in his bare feet. He was quite worried. His roommate was there when he went to sleep last night but gone when the bell sounded this morning. I sent him into the parlor to have a cup of tea and calm his mind."

The senior monks wore identical nonplussed expressions.

"Perhaps he needed some time alone before we begin this most serious week of quiet contemplation," Sanjeev suggested.

"Or perhaps he's in the bathroom," Matsuo offered.

Bodhi knew as well as they did that the missing man might well have changed his mind about seven days of silent meditation. At most retreats, at least one person would leave before the end. In his experience, the breaking point usually came for someone on the third or fourth day. Although he supposed a particularly anxious sort of person might panic before the retreat officially began and run off.

"Or he did, in fact, leave," Sanjeev acknowledged. "That, too, is fine."

"The retreat is for those who are willing," Matsuo finished.

Feng opened his mouth as if to argue then clamped it shut and bowed deeply before backing out of the door, presumably to return to his vegetable-gathering duties. He pulled the door shut gently as he left.

In unison, the two teachers each took a deep breath. They filled their lungs and picked up their knives. Bodhi resumed his chopping.

After finishing his work in the kitchen, Bodhi had time to spare before the sitting meditation began. He walked out the back door and went first to the labyrinth, circling within the low stone walls slowly and watching his feet carry him along dusty spirals cut into the earth.

Then, eager to warm his muscles before an hour of sitting cross-legged on the farmhouse floor, he decided to take a brisker walk. He wended his way through the meadow beyond the maze. It was tall with drying wildflowers and pods at this time of year. But he could envision it as it must be in the high summer, alive with the songs of bumblebees, butterflies, and dragonflies, the sweet fragrance of honeysuckle, and the riotous colors of the flowers and grass.

He followed a sort of rough path carved into the grass by feet that had come before his. The long grass lay trampled and flattened in a more or less diagonal line leading to the road.

He found the body near an old, wide tree stump. At

first, he wasn't sure what he was seeing. But as he drew closer to the lumpy shape on the ground, he knew before he knew.

His heart ticked up. His pulse jumped. And the hair on his arms prickled with electricity. Then his brain processed what his body had already divined. The shape near the tree stump was a man, lying face down in a patch of scrubby grass.

Bodhi covered the rest of the distance at a sprint. He rolled the man to his back and stared down at his slack face. Eyes open and staring sightlessly. Lips already blue. And a thin line of dried blood dotting his neck, which was banded with livid bruises.

Bodhi automatically came to a preliminary determination of cause of death: asphyxia caused by ligature strangulation. The man had been garroted. The primitive garrote, a length of fishing line attached to two sticks, rested neatly on the tree stump.

Bodhi's stomach lurched. The Prairie Center was a place of peace. Now, it had been stained with violence of the worst kind—murder. He turned in a slow circle. The body would not be visible from the street or the house. The murder weapon was brutally efficient. The man would have been overcome from behind, struggled briefly and died quickly. Those were marks of a professional killer.

And yet, the scene felt improvised. No real effort had been made to conceal the body. The weapon had been left behind, as if the killer had fled in a hurry.

He searched the man's blank face carefully, but couldn't place him. If he was a visitor, he was someone Bodhi had never crossed paths with before. He searched the man's pockets. They were all empty. He carried no identification and wore no jewelry and no watch. His clothing was damp with dew.

Bodhi stared down at the man for a moment longer. Then he turned and scanned the gardens outside the kitchen. Feng had moved from the vegetable garden to the herb garden.

He ran toward the monk. "Feng," he called, waving his arms over his head wildly as he raced across the lawn.

The monk looked up at him with a small quizzical frown. "Yes?"

He skidded to a stop at the entrance to the garden and gasped, "The guest who went missing—was he Asian? Chinese, maybe?"

Feng shook his head. The shears in his hand swung from side to side in time with his head. "No. Why?"

Bodhi blinked. He was so sure he'd found the missing student. "What? He's not?"

"No. He's ... I don't know, Eastern European or maybe Russian?"

"Has he come back?"

Feng snipped several stems of lemongrass and placed them in the small basket that hung over the crook of his elbow before answering.

"No. But Bhikkhu Sanjeev says his suitcase is still in the closet, so perhaps he'll return." He shrugged and returned to his work.

Perhaps he would. But, then, who was the dead man in the field?

After a moment, Feng raised his head again. "We do have an Asian man staying here, though. He didn't come for the retreat—he showed up a few weeks ago."

Bodhi's heart thumped against his rib cage. "What's his name?"

"I don't know it."

CHAPTER SIX

Bette was at Durbin's Organic Farm, picking up her fresh eggs, when the call came over her radio.

"Chief, we've got a body at that Buddhist center." The dispatch operator's voice crackled over the radio.

Bette grimaced at Jason's oldest daughter, Claire, and shoved a ten-dollar bill into her hand.

"Wait, Chief Clark. I have to give you your change!"

Bette waved a hand over her shoulder as she jogged down the muddy hill to her car with the carton of eighteen eggs tucked under her arm. "Keep it," she called.

She fiddled with the radio with her free hand as she slid the eggs into the footwell of the passenger side of the car for safekeeping.

"Kelly, please confirm the location for me. There's a body at The Prairie Center?"

"Yes, ma'am. Not in the house, though—out in the field."

Bette swore under her breath. "One of the monks?"

"No, ma'am. Sounds like a John Doe."

"Thanks, Kelly. I'm headed there now."

She buckled her seatbelt, raised her travel mug of coffee to her lips, and bumped along the rutted path leading from the Durbins' farm to the county road.

Her mind rolled through her mental compendium of interactions with the Buddhists. They were usually quiet. No complaints, no issues. They didn't call when hunters trespassed on their land. They didn't have domestic disputes. They opened their doors to the locals every other month for a potluck meal and religious lecture and they sponsored one of the ten-and-under baseball teams. They were the quintessential good neighbors.

She sped up and passed Tucker Rogers, who was towing a thresher behind his pickup. The threshing machine didn't seemed to be well secured to the trailer, so she was happy to see Tuck was using his hazards and driving at a conservative twenty miles per hour. She offered up a silent prayer that he made it all the way home with the machinery.

She pulled into the driveway and parked about a third of the way up. If the body was in the field, there was no point in driving all the way up to the house. As she killed the engine, a robed figure stepped down from the porch and started to walk in her direction.

She shielded her eyes with a hand and squinted at him to see whether it was Matsuo, the Japanese monk, or Sanjeev, the one from Sri Lanka. The man beamed a smile at her in greeting as he tripped hurriedly down the driveway. Matsuo.

"Morning, Matsuo."

He nodded gravely. "For some, a good morning. For others, perhaps not."

She couldn't argue that point. "So, who died?"

"We're not sure."

"Excuse me?"

"The man was staying with us, but we don't know his name."

Bette let her eyebrows shoot up her forehead and gave Matsuo her best skeptical face.

"It's true. He's Chinese and, as far as we know, he didn't speak any English. He showed up two weeks ago with two visitors who said they'd met him at a coffee shop in Elm."

"Did he speak English then?"

Matsuo laughed weakly. "No, he approached them at the counter and showed them one of our brochures.

He likely assumed they were headed here by their appearances."

That part was believable. She was usually able to pick out The Prairie Center's guests when they came into town. There was something about the way they carried themselves. That, and the scent of patchouli that traveled around them in a cloud.

"So you opened your doors to some guy who spoke no English and didn't ask him for any identification or a credit card or anything?"

"Of course we did."

Of course they did.

"Okay, well, he's not getting any younger out there. Let's go have a look."

He coughed. "So, here's the thing. We're hosting a week-long silent retreat. It just started this morning. Sanjeev and I were planning to address the guests in a joint Dharma talk after their sitting meditation ends. Could I send you out to the field with the man who found the body instead?"

"Well, I suppose so. As long as he speaks English."

Matsuo smiled and bowed. "Dr. King speaks English very well. Thank you for accommodating me in this way. Please stop in for some tea when you've finished up, if you like." He turned and gestured to a man standing near the steps to the porch.

She managed to stifle the sarcastic comment that bubbled to her lips as the monk walked away. If Matsuo thought she was finished with him, he was sadly mistaken. A person couldn't just delegate away a dead Chinese guy in his field. That wasn't how any of this worked.

Dr. King strode toward her. He was tall and thin, with unruly curly hair and bright, alert eyes. He was wearing street clothes—tan pants and a black long-sleeve shirt and, despite the chill, sandals. He approached her with his hand outstretched.

"Chief Clark, I'm Bodhi King." His hand was warm and his handshake firm, but not bone-crushing.

"Matsuo said you're a doctor?"

"I'm a retired forensic pathologist—I do some consulting here and there."

"So a medical examiner found my body?"

"More or less."

"Handy."

"I was taking a walk and just sort of ... stumbled over him. Over there, in the meadow." He pointed toward the high grass near the road.

"Lead the way."

As she fell into step beside him, she took a discreet sniff. No patchouli. He smelled like soap and cedar. But maybe her sniff was less subtle than she'd thought because he gave her a sidelong look.

He stepped over a knee-high patch of Bluestar plants. She noted that he was careful not to trample the wildflowers. He led her toward a line of trees, and she spotted the body near an old stump.

"Did you touch it?"

"Yes. He was on his stomach. I turned him over to check for a pulse."

Her eyes moved to his face. "I realize you didn't do an examination. But do you have any thoughts on cause of death?" She waited for him to say 'heart attack' or 'he tripped and hit his head.'

"Ligature strangulation."

She felt her eyes go wide. "He was strangled?"

"Garroted, to be precise."

She shook her head, not believing what she was hearing. "That can't be."

"I'm afraid it is. The murder weapon's right there on the stump."

Bette stepped around the body, averting her eyes, and made a beeline for the garrote. Dried blood was flaking off the fishing line and falling on to the stump.

"You didn't touch this, did you?"

"No." He responded from beside the body.

She took one last look at the garrote then forced

herself to join him at the corpse. She'd seen her share of dead people—usually, crash victims; the occasional fatal farm machinery accident; and a handful of deaths by natural causes she'd encountered in the course of well-being checks. But murder didn't often come to call in Onatah, Illinois. She'd only investigated a single homicide, and that had been when she was a rookie cop, right out of the police academy.

No need to let the forensic pathology consultant know that, though. She reached into her pocket and pulled out the pair of gloves she'd taken from the kit in her car. As she snapped them on, he nodded approvingly.

"I'm sorry I don't have a pair of my own," he said. "It's not the sort of thing I'd pack for a silent retreat."

"I'd be worried if you had."

He laughed politely. Then he gestured for her to crouch next to him. She squatted and sank back on her heels. He pointed at the man's neck.

"The bruising above the indention left by the wire indicates the perpetrator looped the wire around his neck from behind and held it tight until he asphyxiated."

"Would it have taken long?"

"Probably not. And there's a good chance he lost consciousness before he died."

She figured that was a small mercy. She stared down at the dead stranger.

"Your monk says nobody knows who this guy is."

He nodded. "That's what he told me, too. I guess this man came in a few weeks ago, with some travelers who've since moved on. He kept to himself, which isn't all that unusual. But aside from the monks who live here and maybe one or two others, most of the people staying at the center right now only arrived within the last twenty-four hours—including me. I doubt he had time to make any friends."

"You really want to go a week without talking?"

"Wanted to. The plan seems to have changed seeing as how I'm out here talking to you and not inside on my cushion."

She stood and brushed her hands on her pants then regarded him closely. "I'm going to need to talk to everyone in the house. You know that, right?"

B odhi sized up the police chief. From their limited interactions, he could see she was smart and direct. He assumed she was also tough, given the nature of her job.

"I understand you have an unidentified murdered

victim." He paused, then said, "Please don't think I'm trying to tell you how to run your investigation. I wouldn't dream of doing that."

"Good."

"But if I could offer a couple suggestions?"

"Go ahead," she said in a cautious tone.

"Let me act as liaison between you and the center."

She began to shake her head before he finished the sentence. "Out of the question."

"Hear me out, please. Matsuo and Sanjeev are spiritual leaders. So, while they owe you and the community a duty to answer your questions and cooperate with your investigation, they also have a duty to the students who are staying at the center. And I think you know which one will control."

"If they obstruct my investigation, they'll regret it."

"That's not what I'm saying. I'm saying the best way to approach them is with some finesse—not that you don't have finesse," he hurried to correct himself.

"Hah. No one's ever accused me of finesse before. But I *can* be diplomatic, Dr. King. Believe me. I wouldn't have lasted as long as I have in what's essentially a political position without possessing some tact."

"I don't doubt it. But, unless I'm mistaken, you're not well-acquainted with Buddhist teachings."

She conceded the point. "No, I'm not."

"If you push them, Sanjeev and Matsuo *will* flout your law in the service of a higher law. And then, nobody wins. If you let me help you, it'll be easier for you and for them. I mean, who better to facilitate the investigation of a murder that occurred on the grounds of a Buddhist retreat center than a forensic pathologist who happens to be a Buddhist?"

Her eyes narrowed. "Are you?"

"Am I what?"

"Are you a forensic pathologist who happens to be a Buddhist or are you a Buddhist who happens to be a forensic pathologist?"

He started to answer, then paused. "Is there a difference?"

"I think there might be." She kicked at the dirt with the toe of her shoe. "But I don't know that I have much of a choice. Aside from your relationship with the monks, I have to face reality. Onatah doesn't have its own coroner. We share one with Elm and Creekview."

"That's fairly common," he assured her.

"Yeah? Well, our shared coroner isn't a medical doctor."

"Veterinarian?" he guessed. That wasn't unheard of.

"Nope. Butcher."

Okay, *that* was unusual. "Oh."

"So, you've got a deal, Dr. King. But if I get so much

of an inkling that you're not playing straight or you're trying to protect your spiritual leaders, our deal's off." She stuck out her hand.

He shook it. Then he shivered as a cold breeze swept across the prairie, chilling his bare ankles. "Deal."

CHAPTER SEVEN

Hannah Lee Lin frowned down at the corn kernel. She'd been frowning at the blasted thing off and on for two days. It simply wasn't a Supra Seed product—she'd recognize it if it were.

She hoped against all reason that at the meeting earlier this morning, someone would casually toss out a mention of some top-secret experimental strain that she'd never heard of.

But that bit of wishful thinking hadn't come to pass. For one thing, everyone at the meeting had been obsessing over the Crop-Clear issue. Apparently, the affected farmers were threatening to band together and file a class action lawsuit. The legal team had given a grim presentation about the potential scope of damages.

For another thing, it would be impossible for the company to create a new seed without involving her. She wasn't the most senior person in the research and development department, but she *was* the most experienced plant pathologist in the company. Supra Seed simply wouldn't develop a product without her input. They paid her enough for it, they'd use it.

She picked up the seed and turned it between her thumb and forefinger, staring at it from every angle. It was a basic principle of corn genetics that every ear of corn held multitudes. Each tiny kernel was a unique offspring, with its own genotype and phenotype, potentially different from the rows and rows of siblings with which it shared a stalk. Despite that, the kernels could only be the product of the genes they had inherited from their parents. And this seed did not have parents she recognized. It was the wrong color, the wrong shape. It was all wrong.

Unless ...

She dropped the kernel back to the surface of her metal desk and gripped the edge of the desk, using it to push off. Her chair shot backward, rolling across the room until it banged to a stop against the locked cabinets that lined the wall under the window.

Could the strange kernel be a genetic mutant that

had changed in response to disease or pesticide or some other environmental stressor? Could it have evolved after an infection?

She unlocked a drawer and flipped through the plastic sleeves she kept under lock and key. Any one of the samples in the drawer could wipe out every seedling currently growing in the lab. Fungi, bacteria, weeds, toxins. All devastating, all robust, but none that would account for the appearance of the kernel on her desk.

So where had it come from? And how?

Was this new seed the result of some as yet-undiscovered signaling pathway? She'd heard recently that a new pathway was believed to be responsible for increased yield. Perhaps a similar mechanism explained this kernel.

She shook her head. She'd have to ask a geneticist if she really wanted to know. And doing so would invite questions she didn't want to answer—couldn't answer.

No, she'd have to tease out the answer on her own.

She needed more information, though.

She closed the drawer and locked it. She stood and pulled the cord to lower the blind on her left window so that it stopped exactly one third of the way down. She idly noted the glow from one of the tall halogen lights that towered over the parking area wash over one of the omnipresent security SUVs that patrolled the perimeter just inside the gated entrance to the campus. Then she walked over to the right window and lowered its blind so that it covered the entire glass.

She'd get her answers—one way or another.

She traded her white laboratory coat for her warm purple jacket, which she belted tightly around her waist before hanging the lab coat neatly on the hook on her office door. Then she powered down her laptop, gathered her purse and keys, and turned to leave.

The seed of corn on her desk caught her eye. She huffed out a breath and swept it back into its small envelope. She opened the top desk drawer and hesitated, her hand hovering over the tray.

Just drop it in the drawer, she told herself. Removing a seed from the building was a fireable—not to mention, criminal—offense. It was presumptive evidence of corporate espionage. If she was stopped, she couldn't exactly explain that she'd brought the seed from home. That would expose her to a line of inquiry she definitely wanted to avoid.

And yet, it felt wrong to leave the seed there. It didn't belong—she knew it in her heart. And the risk that it could somehow get mixed into Supra Seed's careful breeding program and wreak havoc on their plans to feed starving global populations was too much to bear. She'd barely slept last night, worrying over it.

She slammed the drawer shut and slid the envelope into her jacket pocket, ignoring the *rat-a-tat* drumbeat of her heart, and marched out of the office before she lost her nerve. She didn't stop to turn out the lights.

CHAPTER EIGHT

9:00 P.M.

Bodhi waited until after the evening Dharma talk to approach Sanjeev. Although he was, by necessity, not observing the rules regarding silence himself, he saw no reason to be disrespectful to the other retreat attendees. After the Dharma talk and before the final meditation bell sounded, the guests were welcome to discuss their progress with the monks, read, or otherwise attend to personal needs.

Bodhi's personal need was information. So, he lingered in the warm, dimly lit study after the session broke up, studying the titles on the spines of the books that lined the shelves until the last guest bowed to Bhikkhu Sanjeev and took his leave.

"Come, let's talk by the fire," the monk said, flashing Bodhi a knowing look.

He abandoned the pretense that he was perusing the bookshelves and joined Sanjeev at a pair of chairs in front of the hearth.

"I enjoyed your Dharma talk."

The monk bobbed his head. "Thank you. But you don't want to talk to me about the five *niyamas*, do you?"

Bodhi smiled. "No, not really." Although he'd long been fascinated by the Theravada interpretations of the five natural laws that governed the universe, he was currently more interested in learning about the murder victim he'd nearly tripped over during his morning walk.

Sanjeev seemed to read his mind. "I'm afraid I don't know who that unfortunate man in the field was."

"I think that was by design, *bhante*."

"What do you mean?" Sanjeev wrinkled his brow.

"Someone—he, himself, I imagine—went to a great deal of trouble to render him unknowable." He recalled the findings he'd made in the space Chief Clark had managed to secure for him in the morgue of the county hospital. "The labels had been removed from all his clothes—including his underpants and shoes. He carried no personal effects, jewelry, or identification. His finger-prints were ... obscured."

The monk blinked rapidly. "Obscured?"

"They were deliberately altered. Every finger of each hand has a deep z-shaped cut across it. If his finger-prints are in any database—and if he went through the trouble to do this, you can assume they are—the cuts will interrupt the pattern and basically confuse the algorithm that's trying to match his prints against the samples in the database. It's crude, it calls attention to the fact that someone is trying to evade detection, but it's ultimately effective," Bodhi explained. *Especially when the person is dead and can't be questioned,* he added silently.

"And the ... murderer ... didn't do this? This man did this to himself?"

"They're not new cuts."

"Hmm."

They sat in silence for a moment. Bodhi allowed his heavy eyes to be drawn to the dancing flames in the fire-place. After a long travel day yesterday, he'd planned to spend the day meditating and listening, not performing an autopsy and gathering forensic evidence.

He didn't realize his eyelids had fluttered closed until he heard Sanjeev cough discreetly, twice. He opened his eyes.

"Do you think this man was a criminal, running from

the law?" the teacher asked in a voice that quavered almost imperceptibly.

"Possibly. Did any of the monks or early arrivals for the retreat talk to him that you noticed?"

"No. He didn't seem to speak English. Or Japanese. Or Tamil or Sinhalese, or any of the languages anybody here speaks."

"That's convenient."

The monk shrugged. "Matsuo knows a few words of Tibetan and a few more of Mandarin. But when he tried to speak to the man, he answered in Cantonese. But, in the end, it didn't seem important. People who come here don't really need to be able to communicate with us. They simply need to be able to be still. Sometimes that's more readily achieved when there's a language barrier."

"Could he have been pretending not to understand or speak English?"

"I suppose he could have been. But why would he?"

Bodhi didn't have an answer for that, so he asked his next question. "May I see his belongings? Did he have a suitcase or bag?"

Sanjeev frowned thoughtfully. "He had a small pack. It was leather, so we showed him a place to store it in the old barn behind the garden. You're welcome to take it to the police. But please don't bring it into the house."

"Of course not." The monks were strict vegans. Animal hide would be an upsetting and discordant addition to their household. "I'll take it into town in the morning."

Sanjeev shifted forward, preparing to stand. "If there's nothing else, Bodhi, I'd like to check in on a few of our friends who are struggling with their practice—before the noble silence begins."

"One last question?"

His teacher acquiesced with a brief nod.

"Thank you. The guest who disappeared this morning, Feng said he left behind his bags, as well. Has he returned?"

"Not yet."

Bodhi could see the question forming in Sanjeev's eyes. He watched the monk wrestle with whether to ask it. Finally, he did, forcing the words out in a strange staccato rhythm.

"You don't think there's any connection between the man who left and the ... murder?"

"I don't know," he answered honestly. "I hope not."

If one of the guests of The Prairie Center had killed a fellow enlightenment seeker, it would be a terrible blow to the community. It seemed almost unimaginable. And, yet, Bodhi's imagination made room for the possibility. It was too neat, one guest vanishing on the same day another was found murdered.

"We can hope, but the reality will be what it is. If he's not back by morning, perhaps you should have a look at his things as well, Bodhi." Sanjeev's voice was dull and heavy. He stood and nodded his good night.

"Sleep well."

"Sleep peacefully." Sanjeev left the room on silent feet.

Bodhi stared into the fire, thinking.

CHAPTER NINE

Wednesday morning

Bette was considering whether to walk across the street to the bakery for a muffin when her secretary buzzed her to let her know she had a visitor.

"Chief, there's a Dr. King here to see you."

"Thanks, Lindsey. Send him back."

She shoved her files into an approximation of order and swept the pile of junk mail into her recycling bin. Good enough.

Bodhi appeared in the doorway, holding a leather drawstring rucksack in one hand and a white bakery bag in the other.

"Hi." He walked into the room and handed her the pastry bag. "I brought you breakfast to thank you for getting me credentialed at the morgue yesterday. You cut through red tape faster than anyone I've ever met."

"I have my ways." She peeked into the paper bag. "A blueberry honey muffin. How'd you know those are my favorite?"

"I have my ways." He smiled slyly. "Also, I asked the woman behind the counter what she would recommend as a bribe for the chief law enforcement officer in town."

She broke off a corner of the muffin and popped it into her mouth. There was just something about the bright tang of the berries and the lazy sweetness of the honey that made the perfect taste combination.

After she'd savored that first bite, she squinted at him. "Bribe? I thought this was a thank you gift."

"It's a little of both. I need another favor." He hefted the leather bag. "This belonged to our John Doe."

She dropped the muffin back into the bag and abandoned it on her desk. "Really? That's great."

She walked around her desk, eager for a look at the contents of the bag.

"Don't get too excited," he warned.

He handed her the bag. She pulled the drawstring and peered inside. The smell of aged leather filled her nose. She felt around the bag. There was nothing in it.

"It's empty?" She looked up at him in disbelief.

"Completely. And, just like his clothing, the label's been removed."

"Who travels with an empty bag?"

"Nobody."

"But, he did have clothes, shampoo, toothpaste, things like that, right?"

"Apparently. Presumably he had some money, too."

"What the devil's going on?"

He shook his head sadly. "I'm as confused as you are. I spoke to Matsuo this morning. The man definitely didn't wear the same clothes every day. And he attended to his hygiene, so he had personal items in this bag at one point."

"So where are they?"

"The monks don't know."

Anger flared in her belly. "Don't know or won't say? What are they hiding?"

"I honestly don't think Matsuo or Sanjeev are hiding anything. But someone is."

She clenched her teeth. "When are we going to catch a break in this investigation?" she muttered more to herself than to him.

"There's a second guest who's gone missing." His voice was soft.

She gripped the bag. "Disappeared? Have you checked the field?"

"Actually, I have—no bodies today."

"Thank goodness for small favors," she said dryly.

"But I don't think he's dead. The monks believe this man may have decided a week of silence wasn't up his alley."

"So he just took off?"

"It happens."

That was no surprise. She'd be climbing the walls by the end of the first silent day.

She studied his face. "But you don't think that's what happened, do you?"

"He left behind a suitcase."

"Wait, let me guess. Empty?"

"No, this one wasn't empty. It held sort of the usual things—clothes, an extra pair of shoes, hat and gloves. Some books, an envelope of cash. Toiletries."

"Does this guy have a name?"

"The name on his luggage tag says Boris Badenov."

Finally, an actual lead. She grinned. "Great. Maybe if he's not dead, too, we have our killer."

"Let's not get ahead of ourselves. Besides, I'm pretty sure it's an alias."

"An alias," she repeated slowly. "What makes you think so?"

"Didn't you watch television growing up? Boris

Badenov? Boris and Natasha? He's the bad guy from The Rocky and Bullwinkle Show."

She stared at him as her excitement drained away. "You've got to be kidding me." It came out as a growl.

He widened his eyes and arranged his expression into an apology. "Maybe have another bite of your muffin?" he suggested.

The mention of the pastry reminded her of his bribery comment. "Wait. What's the favor?"

"Okay." He filled his lungs, exhaled slowly, then said, "I think you should call in the feds—"

"No."

"Hear me out. I know they can be a pain in the butt. Believe me, I realize what I'm suggesting."

"Then why even bring it up? It's out of the question." She jabbed a finger at him for emphasis.

"Chief Clark, they have tools that would prove helpful. Look at what we have. A dead Chinese man, with no identification, no name, no fingerprints. A missing Eastern European traveling under the name of a cartoon spy. This most likely isn't a local issue."

"I can handle a dead guy and a missing guy. Just because they're not a pair of blond, corn-fed farmers doesn't change anything."

He held up his hands as if to ward off the lecture, but she was just getting warmed up.

"And if you think—"

She would have lit into him, but at that moment, Lindsey flew into the room, breathless and shaky. "Chief, Mark Olson's fields are burning."

Bette's heart leapt out of her chest and landed in her throat. For a moment, she couldn't speak. When the initial surge of adrenaline waned, she barked out orders. "Call Kevin at the fire department. The Olsons probably already called, but do it just in case. Then call Supra Seed. Mark's growing an experimental seed in one of his fields. They'll want to protect their investment, so they might send someone over to help."

Lindsey nodded and hurried out of the room.

"Put the volunteers on notice, too," Bette called after her.

Then she turned to Bodhi. "This conversation's not over," she warned.

She dropped the leather bag, grabbed her gun, radio, and keys, and raced out the door.

CHAPTER TEN

fter Bette Clark ran out and left him in her office, Bodhi took a moment to consider his next steps. He hadn't expected the police chief to agree to call in the FBI the first time he made the suggestion. But he remained convinced it was the right choice. He'd just need to lead her to it obliquely.

For now, he supposed he could find a ride to the hospital and check on the status of the John Doe's blood and tissue samples. He scooped the bag up from the floor where Chief Clark had left it and started down the hallway to Lindsey's desk to see if she could arrange a lift to the morgue.

But Lindsey was nowhere in sight. Her chair was empty and her computer monitor's screensaver danced across the screen. He lingered at her desk for a few moments but she didn't return. He could walk, he knew, but that would take the better part of his morning. He stepped out into the parking lot and pulled out his phone to check whether any of the ride sharing startups operated in the greater Onatah area.

He leaned against the brick exterior of the building and searched for his current zip code to see if there was a car available in the area. The hum of an engine caught his attention. A dark sedan turned off Main Street and drove into the lot, fast. Without slowing, the driver headed straight toward him and came to an abrupt stop just feet away.

The driver was male, somewhere between thirty-five and forty, with close-cropped, almost military, hair. He wore mirrored sunglasses even though the day was overcast. A blonde woman, her straight hair pulled into a tight low bun, matching sunglasses covering her eyes, practically bolted from the passenger seat.

"Dr. Bodhi King?" she called as she walked toward him at a rapid clip.

"Um ... yes."

"We'd like a word." She gestured toward the still-idling car. The driver gave him a brisk nod.

"And you are?"

"Agent Clausen. That's Agent Thurman behind the wheel."

Agents.

"Are you guys from the FBI?" Maybe he wouldn't have to convince Chief Clark to make any calls after all.

Clausen cocked her head and frowned at him. "FBI? No. Sir, would you join us in the car, please?"

Despite the interrogative sentence structure, she clearly wasn't asking. He considered his options.

"I'd be happy to, Agent Clausen. But I'd like to know what this is about—and what agency you and your friend are with—before I do so. Oh, and I'll need a ride to the county hospital."

Her eyebrows shot up to her hairline. "Anything else? Shoe shine? Latte?"

He pretended her sarcasm was lost on him. "Nope, that's all." He smiled warmly.

She snorted.

He waited.

Her eyes shifted to the car. Bodhi didn't imagine she and her partner could possibly be communicating nonverbally, what with the sunglasses, but after a few seconds, Agent Thurman raised his shoulders then let them fall.

Apparently the shrug spoke volumes. Clausen pushed her sunglasses up to the top of her head and pierced him with cornflower blue eyes.

"We're ODNI, specifically we're currently attached to the NCSC."

None of the letters meant anything to him. For a moment, he wondered if they worked for one of the so-called 'shadow' agencies. An old pal of his from Pittsburgh, a one-time member of the Department of Homeland Security, now worked for a mysterious agency that seemed not to officially exist.

But after a moment, Clausen clarified, "We're career agents with the Office of the Director of National Intelligence working on a matter for the National Counterintelligence Security Center, Dr. King."

Well that all sounded very official—and important. "I see. What about the lift?"

"Does it look like we're running a taxi service?"

"Look, presumably you want to talk about the dead body I found, right?"

She whipped her head around as if someone might overhear. He didn't want to be the one to break it to her, but there wasn't a breathing soul in Onatah, Elm, or any of the adjacent towns who hadn't already heard that some doctor from Pittsburgh stumbled over a murder victim while taking a walk at The Prairie Center.

"Yes," she hissed.

"Great. If you drive me to the morgue, I'll show him to you."

She let out a breath that sounded like air escaping

from a balloon. "Fine. Now will you please get in the car?"

"Sure."

"Your chariot awaits."

He followed her to the car's rear passenger side door. She yanked it open and ushered him inside with an exaggerated flourish.

He settled himself in the back seat. The interior was overheated and smelled strongly of some woodsy scent.

Thurman twisted in the seat and offered Bodhi his hand.

"Charlie Thurman." His booming voice was cheery, and his handshake was efficient.

"Bodhi King."

"We're taking Dr. King to the hospital," Clausen told him.

"The morgue?"

"Yes."

Thurman nodded. "Great. We can go over the preliminaries en route."

"Unless the aroma of your hair wax overtakes us all," Clausen responded.

"Pomade, Elise. It's called pomade." He looked over the tops of his sunglasses and caught Bodhi's eye in the rearview mirror. "And it's melting because, despite her

Scandinavian roots, Agent Clausen over here insists on cranking the heat."

"Scandinavian roots," Clausen muttered. "As if we all lived in ice houses."

Bodhi observed the banter between the two. Their ribbing was good natured, and it seemed they'd been partners for a while.

After a moment, Clausen cleared her throat. "As you've surmised, Dr. King, we're interested in your John Doe."

"Just out of curiosity, who told you about him? I mean, I know Chief Clark didn't reach out to you. And I doubt very much the monks at The Prairie Center called you."

"You're right. It wasn't the monks, and it sure wasn't Bette Clark," Thurman laughed.

"So ..."

"Supra Seed called the NCSC."

"Charlie," his partner said in a voice that held a warning.

"The man's a forensic pathologist. We're going to ask him questions about the corpse. It's only fair to give him some background."

She clicked her tongue and turned around to glare at Bodhi. "Do you have any federal clearances?"

"Uh, no." He shook his head, too confused by what

Thurman had said to focus on her question. "I'm sorry—the seed company called you about a murder?"

"Yes," Thurman said.

At the same time, Clausen said, "No."

Bodhi shifted in his seat. "I'm getting a vibe that you two aren't on the same page about how much to share with me. And, that's fine. But I'm working this case with Chief Clark, and I'm starting to think we should wrap her into this conversation."

"That's not necessary," Clausen said.

At the same time, Thurman said, "I think that's a good idea."

"Do you two ever talk to each other?" Bodhi asked.

The agents in the front seat exchanged frustrated glares from behind their matching sunglasses. After a long silence, Clausen sighed. "Fine. Sure. Let's invite Chief Clark to the party. Any idea where she is?"

"She left in a hurry. There's a fire at a farm ... let me think for a second ... it was the Olson farm."

Thurman swung the car around in the middle of the road. The tires squealed and the rear end of the car fishtailed.

"What the heck, Charlie!" Clausen gripped the handle on the car's door.

"I guess your people weren't into luging either, huh?" Thurman grinned at her. "Didn't you see all that black smoke when we were driving in to get the doc? Assuming there's only one field currently burning, we drove right past it earlier."

"She's probably kind of busy," Bodhi noted. "It's an active fire."

"This is more important." Any trace of humor had left Thurman's voice. It was suddenly as grim as his partner's face.

Bodhi looked at the cornfields whizzing by outside the window and marveled that the humblest of foods was at the center of this maelstrom.

CHAPTER ELEVEN

To say that Chief Clark wasn't happy to see Bodhi and a pair of federal agents arrive at the scene of the fire was to vastly understate her mood.

She turned toward them as they trudged up the rutted path to the hill where she stood. Behind her, the sky was red and thick with smoke. As far as Bodhi could see, fields were burning. The heat hung heavy on the air, and a sweet, burning smell filled Bodhi's nose.

A pump truck was parked at the crest of the hill. A pair of firefighters trained a hose on the burning crops, and several men in street clothes passed buckets of sloshing water in an assembly line and returned them. A woman in running clothes filled them from the hose attached to the farmhouse.

Chief Clark's eyes flashed. "You can't be serious. You called the FBI?"

"They're not FBI. And I didn't call them. They came looking for me at your office."

She shifted her attention to the pair of agents. "I don't have time for this right now. I'm a little busy," she snapped.

"Chief, respectfully, we're here on a matter of national security. And it looks as though the fire professionals have this situation under control. We need to speak with you." Agent Thurman was polite and respectful, but insistent.

The police chief's face clouded. "The situation is not under control. Not to diminish your *national security concerns*," she said with a barely suppressed sneer, "but Mark Olsen's about to lose his livelihood."

She gestured toward a man in jeans and a long-sleeved shirt. His face was streaked with dirt. His jaw was set. And his bloodshot eyes were clouded with disbelief and pain.

Agents Clausen and Thurman directed their attention elsewhere. They spotted two suited men standing just to the side of the farmer.

The men shared a military bearing, close-cropped hair, and broad shoulders. Bodhi thought they could have been brothers. He also thought they had to be law enforcement.

Clausen nudged Thurman.

Was the fire about to devolve into an interagency jurisdictional squabble? Bodhi'd seen it happen before, under equally grim conditions.

"Excuse us," Clausen said to Bodhi and Chief Clark.

She and her partner strode over to Mark Olson and the two men.

"Get a load of those two," Chief Clark said out of the side of her mouth as they watched the agents walk away. "They forgot about their national security interest pretty fast once they saw who's here."

She seemed to have redirected her ire from Bodhi to the agents, which suited him fine.

"Who *is* here? What agency are they from?"

She laughed shortly. "Those two are former state police. Now they work for Supra Seed as private security. Better pay, better pension, better working conditions."

"They're security guards?"

Another bark of a laugh. "No. They're members of an elite security force that includes former Navy SEALs, Army Rangers, Green Berets, undercover drug enforcement officers, SWAT members, and Lord knows what else."

"For a seed company?"

"For a seed company. You'd be hard pressed to wrap your mind around how big Supra Seed's business is, Dr. King. They provide something like half the world's corn. Most of which is destined for cattle feed. No cattle feed, no beef. They pretty much control the global food supply—or a large portion of it, at least."

Bodhi's eyes widened. "I had no idea."

"Most folks don't. Frick and Frack over there are here to try to save Mark's Maize46 fields. It's an experimental corn hybrid that has a much greater yield and consumes less water, fewer nitrates. It's supposed to be the next big thing. And it's going up in flames."

"They don't seem to be doing much," he observed.

"They've called in a tanker plane to come drop some water on the fields."

"Your county has a firefighting airplane?"

"Are you kidding? The cost would exceed our entire public safety budget. But Supra Seed has one—or maybe two. The folks here on the ground are just trying to keep the fire under control until the plane gets here. Shouldn't be long now."

They lapsed into silence and watched the conversation between the NCSC agents, the security officers, and Mark Olson play out.

The farmer was pointing his finger emphatically.

The four suits were all nodding somberly. The entire cluster turned as one and glanced at the police chief.

She muttered something inaudible as the federal agents returned.

"Mr. Olson believes he knows who started the fire," Clausen announced.

Chief Clark set her lips in a thin line. "I know what he thinks."

"When do you plan to pay a visit to Mr. Durbin, then?" Thurman asked.

"What happened to your national security issue?" she shot back.

"The John Doe's not going anywhere. He'll still be dead tomorrow. But if Jason Durbin destroyed Supra Seed's research crop, you need to bring him in. Now." Clausen's voice rang with urgency.

"Listen here, Agent ..."

"Clausen." she supplied.

"Agent Clausen, Mark's in a state. It's understand-able. And he and Jason have a history. There's bad blood between them. But there's no evidence Jason set this fire, and frankly, I don't believe he did. Mark's grasping at straws for someone to blame."

"So you're not going to investigate?" Thurman pressed.

She shot him a sour look. "I don't know how your

agency operates, but around here we don't haul people in for questioning without a reason. If and when the fire chief tells me that this fire was arson, I'll talk to Jason—among others. But not before."

Clausen frowned. "At a minimum, you need to sit on this Durbin guy. If he did set the fire, he might run. Send a squad car over to his place to park at the end of his driveway."

Bodhi could tell she was trying to compromise. Chief Clark either didn't realize or didn't care.

She threw her head back and laughed. "As if I had a car to spare. I can't have one of my three officers sit there twiddling his thumbs all day. And the notion that Jason Durbin's a flight risk ..." She wiped her eyes before continuing. "He has a ten-acre organic vegetable farm and a flock of free-range layers. And a bunch of bee hives to tend. Not to mention a teenaged daughter and a ten-year-old son. He's not going anywhere. And he's too busy working his tail off to be sneaking around, setting fires."

"All the same—"

"His wife was over here earlier. She brought a thermos of coffee and a pitcher of ice water for the volunteers. Sure, the Durbins and the Olsons have had their differences. But they're neighbors. I don't know where you're from, but around here, we all know each other. Jason Durbin didn't set this fire. If you want to have someone watch his house, ask the fellas from the seed company. Now, if you'll excuse me, I'm busy."

Chief Clark walked away from the agents. They exchanged glances, and Thurman ran after her.

Clausen turned to Bodhi and sighed. "This fire changes things. We're going to need to go talk to the executives at Supra Seed. But don't leave town. The unidentified murder victim is still on our list."

"I'm not going anywhere, other than to the hospital morgue, eventually. I'm staying at The Prairie Center, which I bet you already knew. Chief Clark has my cell phone number. You can reach me through her."

"Or you could just give me the number," Clausen said coolly.

"I could. But you should think of me as a neutral player—I don't have any allegiance to either you or her. All the same, I'm not interested in being party to any end runs around local law enforcement. You and Agent Thurman need to hammer out some ground rules with Chief Clark before you come looking for me again."

Her nostrils flared, but she gave no other outward sign of anger.

He smiled at her. "I'm not trying to make your job

more difficult. I just have no desire to find myself in the middle of a morass."

"Too late," she called after him as he walked back down the hill.

CHAPTER TWELVE

B odhi walked back to The Prairie Center. The smell of burnt hair—the corn silks, he figured— followed him all the way, like a puppy nipping at his heels. Not a single plant pathologist with a black belt happened by to offer him a ride.

By the time he reached the main house, the students were eating lunch. He washed his hands at the kitchen sink and carried a bowl of vegetable stew and brown rice from the kitchen to the long communal table. He found an empty seat and joined the silent meal already in progress.

Despite the clunky awkwardness of sharing a meal without conversation, he'd always enjoyed the mindful meals at retreats. The lack of chatter enabled him to truly concentrate on the food in his bowl, but the presence of other people lent a convivial, if quiet, atmosphere. He picked up his spoon and studied the colorful stew.

As he ate, he maintained a leisurely pace and focused principally on the nourishing food the monks had prepared. Sweet carrots, purple potatoes, and late tomatoes from the garden swirled in his bowl with fresh herbs and plump kernels of corn. He found himself wondering where the corn had been grown. He felt sure the monks wouldn't buy corn from Supra Seed. Perhaps Jason Durbin had watered and tended the corn in his stew.

After the meal, Roshi Matsuo announced that the next few hours would be dedicated to working meditation. The students who'd spent most of their morning sitting seemed eager for the more active form of mindfulness.

Bodhi understood the impulse. Sometimes focusing narrowly on a task at hand—washing dishes, sweeping a floor—was a joyful meditation. The job was always what it was, but by bringing attention to it, a person could honor it and enjoy it.

He waited patiently as the senior monks read out names and work assignments. Bhikkhu Sanjeev said his name last.

"Bodhi, we weren't certain you'd be here, so we left a

solitary task for you. You'll be cleaning out the root cellar in the basement." The monk smiled kindly.

Bodhi got the distinct impression that this particular job had just been invented on the fly. But it made no difference. A few hours spent clearing out a basement would also help him to clear his head.

"Yes, *bhante*," he said because it seemed as if the monk was waiting for a response.

Sanjeev glanced at Matsuo, and the Zen teacher handed Bodhi a small glass canning jar and a square of cardstock.

"Spider catcher?" Bodhi guessed.

Matsuo nodded and smiled his beatific smile.

"Thanks." Bodhi swallowed a laugh.

He spent a good bit of his time mucking about inside dead bodies, up to his elbows in blood and viscera. Given the requirements of his day job, he wasn't particularly squeamish and had no difficulty following the Buddha's teaching not to harm any living creature, including insects, rodents, and arachnids.

Besides, he had a suspicion the teachers were playing up the spiders in the basement angle to keep the rookies on their toes. No one ever said Buddhists didn't have a sense of humor.

Three minutes in the basement made it clear that Matsuo and Sanjeev had not been exaggerating the likelihood of spiders. In fact, Bodhi thought, as he scooped up yet another black spider and transported it to the high, small window that opened out into the garden and released the critter, the root cellar cleaning effort might be nothing more than an exercise in spider removal.

He returned to the dimly lit front cellar and took stock of the piles. The best way to clear it out would be to just pick a corner and work his way out of the room. He decided to start in the back right corner and picked his way through some old wooden crates and glass milk bottles.

The corner was occupied by what looked to be a large rectangular piece of furniture—a low coffee table or perhaps a storage trunk—covered with a faded blue blanket. Bodhi removed the blanket and shook out the dust. He pretended not to see the spider that fell out of its folds and skittered across the floor. He set the blanket aside to be laundered and inspected the trunk that had been underneath it.

It wasn't, as he'd thought, a piece of furniture. It was a wheeled foot locker. The sort of thing a teen might take to camp. If he had to guess, he'd venture that one of the novice monks had used it to transport his belongings to the house then had stowed it down here after he'd set up his bedroom. He tried the push button key lock but it was secured.

He turned his attention away from the corner and selected a crate full of vinyl record albums that was next to the locked trunk. Assuming the monks didn't have a record player, they could sell these to a vintage record store, he thought, as he flipped through the album covers. He placed the crate near the doorway.

Returning to the corner, he ducked his head to avoid the bare lightbulb that hung from the stone ceiling into the middle of the root cellar. As he did so, the foot locker caught his attention again.

Forget it. It's locked.

He turned his back and sorted through a haphazard pile of paperbacks—mainly romances, thrillers, and westerns. Not exactly the sorts of books the monks kept in the library, but he'd take them upstairs and see if anybody wanted them. If not, he'd add a stop at a used book store or library donation box to his list of errands.

He stacked the books on top of the records. His thumb caught on a small paperclip that someone had once used to mark his or her page in the book on the top of the pile. He unclipped the paperclip from the thin paper and bounced it in his palm.

He returned to the foot locker and examined the inexpensive lock. He straightened the paper clip and inserted it into the keyhole. The lock resisted his efforts. He removed the paperclip and scanned the bins and boxes.

Under the stairs, behind a cardboard container filled with canning jars and lids, he found a small metal tool-box. He popped it open and selected a small, slotted screwdriver.

The blade fit perfectly into the key hole. He turned the screwdriver ever so slightly to the left, and this time, the lock yielded instantly.

He unlatched the clasp on each end of the trunk and lifted the lid. As soon as he looked inside, he knew. The contents of this trunk had belonged to the dead man he'd found in the meadow.

He inventoried the carefully folded clothes first: Two long-sleeved shirts (one gray, one green); two short-sleeved shirts (one black, one gray); two pairs of pants (both tan); three pairs of underwear (white); three pairs of socks (two black, one white); and one pair of blue-and-white striped pajamas. The brand label and size tag for each item of clothing had been neatly removed, leaving behind only a straight, thin narrow line of fabric as evidence the tag had ever existed.

One knife sheath, leather, the same color as the dead

man's knapsack. It held a seven-inch knife with a sharp, curved blade. He turned the knife in his hand. It glinted in the light thrown by the bulb. He slipped it back into the holder and placed it gingerly on top of the folded clothing.

On the bottom of the trunk, nestled under a toiletry kit that had been emptied of its contents, he found a small, bound journal. A thrill of anticipation ran along his spine.

Was he finally going to learn the dead man's name?

He flipped the book open to the first page and eagerly scanned the lines. The page was filled with letters and numbers— more letters than numbers—filling every line from margin to margin.

He paged through the book. It was three-quarters full. The numbers were Arabic and the letters were Roman, but they didn't form a single word of English. He stared down at the diary—or whatever it was—in disbelief.

It was encrypted.

CHAPTER THIRTEEN

Wednesday night, late

Hannah didn't know what time it was. She'd left her cell phone at home as she'd been instructed to do, and she never wore a watch. All she knew was that it was dark and cool, and the smell of fire lingered on the air. She could almost feel the heat rising off the fields, but she dismissed that as her imagination.

Supra Seed's tanker plane had dumped two loads of water on Mark Olson's fields, totaling nearly fifteen hundred gallons. She'd heard the engineers talking about it. There was no way the ground was still hot. It would be soggy and ashy, but not hot, not even warm.

It was foolish to be out here given the circumstances, she knew. Supra Seed's security teams were likely to be patrolling all night—not just the Olson Farm, but every field in the county where an experimental crop had been planted. The destruction of any more crops would be a terrible blow. The entire company was on edge.

Her own supervisor had called the fire 'a declaration of war' but had been unable to articulate who the enemy might be. A competing seed company? A rogue farmer?

She had her own theory, which she pushed deep down into the recesses of her mind and refused to consider. But the thought resisted being suppressed. It kept worming its way up to her consciousness.

Which was why she was roaming around at this hour, alone, while the rest of the county hunted an arsonist. The only other person stupid enough to be out walking was some guy looking for owls.

She stumbled over the uneven ground, swore, and caught herself. She had to be almost to the field now. She strained to see in the dark.

Yes, there, in the distance, she could make out the sign for the farm stand. Another fifty yards or so and she'd reach the cattle fence. She crouched low and ran, ducking out of sight of anyone who might be watching from the house up on the hill.

When she reached the third fence post from the end, she crouched down and pulled the spike out of the ground. Her hand shook as she opened the hollow container.

She plucked the scrap of paper from inside the tube, but even in the dark she could tell it wasn't an answer. It was her question. The one she'd laboriously written out on Tuesday. After she'd signaled with her office blinds that she was making a drop, she'd sat in the coffee shop in town and worked through the code. It had taken her nearly an hour to craft the three sentences using the process he'd taught her.

Why had he gone dark and silent? Could he possibly have set fire to the field?

No. Why would he? He didn't need to do that—she was giving him what he asked for, what he said the country needed. Then where is he, Hannah? Her inner voice scolded her. *What makes you think you can really trust him? Why did he put that strange seed in the spike? Where did he get it?*

She crumbled her note into a ball and jammed it into her pocket. Then she capped the spike and shoved it back into the ground. She wasn't sure she should even bother—he was probably never coming back. But the dead drop container didn't belong to her, after all. So what else was there to do but put it back?

In a way, it would be a relief to stop all this cloak-and-dagger nonsense. She'd refused to help him in the beginning, but then he'd shown her the photographs. Chinese citizens—men, women, children, all rail-thin from hunger in a country unable to grow enough food to feed its people, increasingly at the mercy of the whims of foreign politicians for their next meal. Living under the constant threat of trade sanctions and embargos. She'd known the only way to erase the memory of the haunted eyes, the visible rib cages, the bent postures of the people of her ancestral land would be to cooperate. So she had.

But now, it seemed, he'd taken a different tack—if he'd started the fire. If not, maybe he had everything he needed and had returned to China. What did she expect, that he'd risk his mission—*their* mission—just to leave her a thank you note in the spike?

She didn't want his gratitude, anyway. She'd helped him in the service of something bigger than him, bigger than both of them. But maybe now she was free.

She turned to start the walk back home, her spirits lighter, her step springier.

Then a man's voice rang out from somewhere inside the cattle fence, angry and close. "Hey, whaddya think you're doing? I have a gun. Now, get the hell off my property!"

Her stomach lurched, her heart thudded, and the ground rose up and whirled around and around. She squeezed her eyes shut against the dizziness. Her blood was pounding; she could hear her pulse echoing in her ears.

She opened her eyes and forced her trembling legs into action. She ran as fast as she could, a dark streak flashing through the night. As she ran, the crack of a rifle sounded in the air. One shot. She half expected her legs to give out, or a hot bullet to explode in her back, or blood to run down the side of her head. But she kept running.

He missed. He missed. He missed.

CHAPTER FOURTEEN

Thursday morning

Bodhi woke before the sun rose, before the morning bell rang. He took the encrypted book out from under his pillow and dressed silently in the dark. Then he walked through the sleeping house and slipped out the kitchen door. He stepped off the porch and reached into the window well on the side of house nearest the garden. He retrieved the knife and the backpack from under the coiled garden hose and slung the bag over his shoulder.

As he walked down the long driveway to the road, the knife jostled inside the bag and bumped up against his back. The rhythmic sensations reminded him with every step that he was carrying a dead man's weapon and code book.

He pulled out his cell phone to call Chief Clark. It was very early, but maybe he could leave a message.

She answered on the first ring.

"This is Clark."

"Good morning. It's Bodhi King. You're up early."

"Jason Durbin was shot and killed last night in his field. I'm at his farm." Her voice was flat. It could have been from lack of sleep, but he suspected it was more than that.

"I'm sorry, Bette." He stumbled over her first name, but it felt right to use it for this purpose. She wasn't just a police chief. She was a human being. And from the sound of it, she was a human being who was suffering.

"Jason had a quick temper, but he was a good man, a sweet man. He didn't deserve to go out this way." Anger crept into her deadened tone.

"Call me when you can," he said. This was not the time to tell her about his discovery in the basement.

"Thurman and Clausen are on their way to pick you up and bring you here. Can you help me with the body?" Her voice nearly broke and she barked out a cough.

"Of course. Does this mean you and the feds have reached a mutual understanding of all our mutual roles?"

"More like it means I have people being murdered and crops burning, and I need all the help I can get."

"Fair enough. Don't forget you also have a missing person."

"Right, Boris Badenov with the cold feet. Clausen and Thurman can fill you in, but they know him. That's why they're in town. I have to go."

"See you as soon as I can, chief."

Bodhi ended the call and reached the mouth of the driveway. He figured the government-issued sedan would be coming from the East, but he wasn't positive. He hesitated for a moment near the mailbox.

Before he stepped to either the right or the left, the dark sedan came into view over the rise. He stood still and waited. Clausen was driving today. She brought the car to a stop beside him.

Thurman gave him a little salute. Neither agent was wearing sunglasses. But then again, the sun hadn't yet managed to crest over the low hills.

Bodhi pulled open the rear passenger side door and climbed into the car. He gently placed the leather bag on the seat beside him.

"Good morning, Dr. King," Clausen said formally.

"Morning," Thurman mumbled around a mouthful of egg sandwich.

"Good morning."

"Charlie, if you get crumbs in the foot well, you're vacuuming this thing." Clausen didn't take her eyes off the road. Her icy exterior seemed extra brittle.

"Elise doesn't like ants. She thinks my eating habits attract them," Thurman explained cheerfully.

"What's in the bag?" Clausen nodded her head toward the back seat.

"A knife and a diary or journal of some kind."

"Not yours, I take it?"

"I assume the dead man's. I found it in a trunk in the basement of the monk's house."

"Does it say anything interesting?"

"Wouldn't know. It's written in some kind of code."

Clausen's eyes flashed interest in the rearview mirror. "What kind of code?"

He shook his head. "No idea. It's not really my area of expertise."

"Luckily for us, it's hers." Thurman jerked a thumb toward his partner.

"Great. You can have a look at it later. So what happened to Jason Durbin?"

Thurman shook his head mournfully but didn't pause in the work he was doing on the breakfast sandwich. "Shot from a distance, looks like. Single shot from a hunting rifle. Right through the gut."

"This happened last night?"

"A call came into the emergency dispatch just before midnight. A woman who didn't give her name. Said she was out taking a nature walk, hoping to see some owls. She heard yelling, then a shot."

"Who's the woman?"

Clausen took over. "The dispatcher said she must have called through a voice-over-Internet program on her computer. The numbers those VOIPs assign aren't permanent. No way to trace it. Well, no easy way for the Onatah PD to do it. *We* could do it."

The NCSC agents exchanged looks.

Bodhi changed the subject. "This woman said she heard yelling? Two people?"

"No. One. A man shouted something like, 'I've got a gun, get off my property,'" Thurman said.

"You think it was Durbin?"

"Most likely."

"Did he have a gun?"

"Sort of. They found him with his kid's BB shooter jammed in his back pocket."

They fell silent. Clausen turned off the county road.

After a moment, Bodhi said, "Chief Clark tells me you're here because of Boris Badenov."

Thurman chucked. "That alias gets me every time. Your missing retreat goer is a mercenary of sorts."

"What sort of mercenary?"

"He's a spy. His real name is Gavriil Fyodorovych. He's former SVR, but he's freelancing now. He operates out of Kazakhstan, sometimes Belarus. He specializes in industrial espionage for hire." Clausen did the explaining in a dry voice.

"What's SVR?"

"The Russian Foreign Intelligence Service. After the Soviet Union dissolved, the KGB was split into two arms, a domestic agency and a foreign agency. He worked for the Russian equivalent of the CIA."

"Why would a former Russian spy be staying at a Buddhist retreat center in central Illinois?" Bodhi asked.

"Corn," Thurman answered.

"Corn?"

"Corn."

Bodhi thought this over. "And your interest in him is—?"

"Classified," Clausen told him.

The car bumped over a small dirt lane and came to a rest beside a hand-painted sign advertising fresh eggs and organic produce. Someone with a measure of artistic talent had done the lettering. The brush strokes had whimsical, tidy swoops and curly tails. The daughter in high school, Bodhi guessed, based on nothing at all.

He leaned forward, orienting himself. The farm stand was just up the hill to the left. To the right, set back several feet from the drainage ditch, a wire fence with wood posts marked off a square cornfield that ran back as far as Bodhi could see. Chief Clark's truck was parked parallel between the fence and the ditch. She stood about twenty feet away, wearing a blue windbreaker and a deep frown. She raised her head at the sound of the car's engine and gave them a short wave of greeting.

They exited the car. Bodhi left the bag on the seat. Clausen pointed up the hill as they walked toward the field where Chief Clark stood, still staring down at something lying between the cornstalks. Not something, Bodhi corrected himself. Someone.

She narrated, "The cornfields end at an asphalt lane that runs up to the house, over to the farm stand, and back to the vegetable gardens and the fenced-in area for the chickens."

"I thought they were free-range." Bodhi had imagined the chickens running freely through the ten acres.

Thurman gave him an indulgent smile. "My folks had chickens. You have to contain them somehow or they'll wander into the road. The Durbins give them a wide swath of grass. It looks like the Durbins also move theirs around every so often, so they can eat some new bugs and crap in a new area."

Clausen wrinkled her nose but made no comment.

"City girl," Thurman whispered loud enough for her to hear.

She ignored him and led their trio into the grass and around to the side of the square that was farthest from the road. A gate was set in the fencing, already unlatched.

Thurman gestured for Bodhi to go through ahead of him, so he did.

They walked through golden stalks of corn that were nearly as tall as Bodhi.

"Isn't it getting kind of late in the season to harvest?"

"It's been a warm autumn," Thurman explained. "By this time of year, the harvest's usually ninety percent complete, if not more. I think at the end of last week, only about sixty-four percent of the corn in the state had been harvested. The Supra Seed farmers growing Maize46 are harvesting late because the company asked them to. For research purposes."

"Jason Durbin was harvesting late because he planted late this year. His wife told us he tried to time his harvest so that he wouldn't have vulnerable plants at the height of spraying season," Clausen added.

"Because of Crop-Clear and the drift," Bodhi guessed, recalling what Hannah Lee Lin had told him.

"That's right." Clausen threw him a surprised look.

They joined the police chief in between two rows of

corn, about twenty yards from the fencerow nearest the road.

"I walked away for a few minutes to use the bathroom," she said without preamble. "And his wife came out here and covered him with the blanket from their bed. She said he looked cold, just laying there on the ground. Did she screw up your forensics?"

Bodhi looked down at the lumpy shape under the soft, gray and white marled blanket. "He was shot in the stomach from a distance, right?"

"Yeah."

He shrugged. Yes, Mrs. Durbin had contaminated the crime scene. But, he suspected draping a blanket over her husband's body had given her some comfort. And the truth was, a rifle wound from a distance didn't lend itself to lots of useful fiber or DNA evidence. At least not usually.

Thurman cleared his throat. "Any word from Mark Olson?"

Clausen turned to Bodhi. "Olson came over here yesterday afternoon and confronted Durbin about the fire. The conversation got ... heated."

"Mark's retained an attorney out of Elm. Any questions need to go through him," Chief Clark announced.

"Just great," Thurman grumbled.

Clausen was more philosophical. "Of course he did. I bet Supra Seed's paying for it, too."

Bodhi returned his attention to the blanket. "I should really get started. Anybody who wants to walk away, this is your chance."

By the time he'd crouched beside the body to remove the blanket, the law enforcement officers were three-quarters of the way to the gate.

CHAPTER FIFTEEN

Gavriil crouched in the barn and watched the activity at the organic farmer's field. The police lady had been there since just after midnight. Even from this distance, she looked drawn and tired.

A car sped past on the road in front of the barn and came to a stop at the side of the road near the crime scene. Three people climbed out. A tall, rangy man with curly hair; an angular blonde woman who vibrated with intensity, and a broad-shouldered, buzz-clipped guy in a suit, who hurriedly shoveled the last bites of his breakfast into his mouth.

He adjusted the focus on his binoculars and followed their progress up the hill.

The woman and the guy in the suit were federal agents, no question. Given the circumstances, he'd have expected the FBI to send in a team, but these two lacked the swagger of FBI agents. There was a certain cerebral quietness to them.

Could they be CIA? But the Central Intelligence Agency claimed not to operate on U.S. soil. He rocked with silent laughter at his own naïveté. Why would he, of all people, trust a spy agency's public positions?

He worried that the lack of sleep might be catching up with him. There was nothing funny about that. He needed to stay sharp until this assignment had reached completion. He reminded himself that it was almost over. Although the dead farmer was going to prove to be a complicating factor. He could feel it.

His eyes drifted back to the tight cluster of people walking out to meet the policewoman in the field. The suits couldn't be CIA. Why would the CIA be poking around in the death of a small family farmer? Department of Homeland Security? But, again, that possibility raised the same question. What interest would they have?

Maybe the recently deceased farmer had been growing weed, he thought impatiently. That might fit. The pair could be agents with the Drug Enforcement Agency.

But who was the other guy? He wasn't a federal agent. His gate was too loose, his posture too relaxed.

And he wasn't a local cop. Gavriil had researched the locals. The lady chief, one Army vet, and two wet-behind-the-ears kids who'd just graduated from the police academy.

He frowned. He didn't like surprises.

And he didn't want any further delays. He hated it here. The days were short, the food was bland, and the people were too friendly. He wanted to go home before the weather grew any colder.

He tracked the trio's movements through the field until they reached the point where the body had fallen. There was a brief conversation. The police chief gestured to the blanket; and the stranger shrugged. Then he crouched beside the corpse. The others walked away.

Gavriil watched as the man removed the blanket from the dead farmer. He knew what would be revealed. He'd already seen it through his tactical binoculars. The bullet had ripped through the farmer's lower abdomen. Based on the amount of blood covering the corpse's pelvis, legs, and the plants where he'd fallen, Gavriil figured the bullet had hit a femoral artery right where it branched down into the thigh.

The curly-haired man leaned forward and examined the gaping wound with a thoughtful expression.

Ah, a medical doctor—the kind who worked with

dead people. Gavriil rolled his shoulders. This man presented no threat to him.

After watching for another couple of minutes, Gavriil lowered the binoculars and rubbed his eyes. He glanced over at the horse blanket he'd spread over a bed of fresh hay in the corner. Maybe just a quick nap. He wouldn't miss anything. The coroner, or whoever he was, would likely take hours to do whatever coroner-type things he intended to do.

He set the alarm on his complicated wristwatch to go off in ninety minutes. Then, out of habit, he took one last look at the subject. The federal agents were getting into their car. The woman was behind the wheel. Then, the passenger door opened. The man jumped out and ran over to the cattle fence cradling something in his arms.

Gavriil rotated the turret to move the rectile and increase the magnification. He read the male agent's lips. 'Almost forgot your bag,' he called out to the doctor. The doctor stood and walked to the fence. The agent handed over a weathered-looking brown leather backpack. The doctor nodded his thanks.

Gavriil nearly dropped the thousand-dollar binoculars. He gripped them tight and stared hard. The doctor was holding the Chinese agent's bag. The Chinese government had sent in a replacement much faster than he'd imagined they could. And a white man with access to law enforcement records, at that.

All thoughts of a nap evaporated. He paced around the barn's low loft. He had to hunch his shoulders and take care not to fall to the ground below, but he needed to move to burn off some of the adrenaline that was spiking in his system.

He'd left that bag where it would be completely safe —or so he'd thought. If the doctor had access to the monk's barn, that was bad. If he had access to the main house, that was catastrophic.

He fumbled for his mobile phone in his pocket. He powered it on and began to call his employer. Then he stopped. He reminded himself his first commander's rule: Don't bring me a problem; bring me a solution.

He returned the phone to his pocket and thought hard. He squeezed his eyes shut and dismissed the first thought that came to mind. His first idea was usually lazy. He'd learned that about himself. He dismissed his second idea, too. That was usually trash. After several quiet moments, he smiled. The third idea, now that was the winner.

First, he had to slip back into the barn and the basement at the monk's place and retrieve what was his. It would take careful planning and execution.

Next, he would have to kill the doctor. And the Chinese woman. There was no room for error.

The matter settled, he stretched and yawned. He clambered across the loft to his makeshift bed and lay flat on his back on the scratchy hay. He pulled the equally scratchy blanket over himself and closed his eyes. Within thirty seconds, his breathing slowed and his heavy eyes closed.

He slept the sound and peaceful sleep of a man with a plan.

CHAPTER SIXTEEN

Hannah lay flat on her back and stared unblinkingly up at the ceiling. She pulled her soft fleece blanket up to her chin and stared some more. She pushed it off and turned on her side. She stared at the wall. She closed her burning eyes, swollen from crying and lack of rest, and willed herself to sleep.

It was no use.

She flopped to her other side and checked the time on the bedside clock. It was nearly seven. The sun was rising. She should be out of the shower by now, eating breakfast.

But there was no way she was going into the laboratory today. She'd nearly been killed less than eight hours ago. She flinched at the memory. The shouted warning, the crack of the gun. The feel of the slick grass, slippery under her feet as she ran. The fear that rose in her throat. And the burnt smell hanging in the air, thick and sickly sweet.

Tears welled in her eyes. She reached to take her cell phone from the charger. Maybe if she spoke to her mother, she'd feel better. She hesitated, her hand hovering over the phone.

If she called, her mother would know she was upset and would press her for the reason. She couldn't tell her mother what had happened without admitting what she'd done.

No. She couldn't tell anybody. She'd take the day off, watch reruns on the science fiction channel, and eat toast and jam. She'd forget all about gunshots in the night, missing secret agents, and fields of burning crops.

She picked up the phone and called her supervisor's line. He wouldn't be pulling into the lot for another twenty minutes, so at least she wouldn't have to talk to him in person.

After his recorded greeting finished, she cleared her throat:

Hi, It's Hannah. I'm not going to be able to make it in today. I feel really lousy. I can't even get out of bed. I'll try to be there tomorrow. In the meantime, I'll keep an eye on my email in case anything urgent comes up. Thanks.

She hadn't rehearsed it, but it was perfect. It was one

hundred percent truthful and defensible. Given all the lying and subterfuge she'd been engaging in, that fact was a small but critical triumph.

She rested the phone on the bedside table and took her laptop from the shelf below the clock and lamp. She powered up the computer so she could sign into the streaming television service. But after keying in her login information and going to her home screen, she forgot all about her science fiction marathon.

The local news feed from her Internet provider popped up as a notification. As she read the first five words of the top headline, her heart skipped a beat: *Onatah Farmer Slain in his Field.*

Her hands trembled. It took her two tries to click on the link for the full story. She read it rapidly. Her stomach lurched as she scanned the short article:

> Jason Durbin, of Onatah, was found dead from a single shotgun wound at the Durbin Organic Farm on County Road 113, just after midnight. An unknown female caller alerted authorities to a shot fired. When the police arrived at the scene, Mr. Durbin was already dead. Onatah Police Chief Bette Clark would not comment on the ongoing investigation but did ask that any citizens with information contact the police department. Mr. Durbin leaves behind a wife, a

sixteen-year-old daughter, and a ten-year-old son. This is a developing story and will be updated.

She covered her mouth with her hand. A man was dead. Because of her. She hadn't known. He'd made no sound when he was hit. She told herself she wouldn't have run if he had. She would have gone to him, tried to stem the flow of blood until help arrived.

She swallowed hard, trying to push back the bile that rose in her throat. She glanced back at the screen, feeling lightheaded. There was a picture to go along with the short article.

A tall, thin man—the medical examiner, presumably —caught mid-motion. He was bending his knees, getting ready to crouch down in the high corn. He was facing away from the camera. Curly hair and a glimpse of an angular jaw were all the photographer caught.

It was odd, she thought, that he wasn't wearing an official navy windbreaker like Chief Clark, captured standing by the fence. She looked again at the curly hair. The casual khaki pants and the long-sleeved shirt. It was Bodhi King, the Buddhist forensic pathologist.

Wheels began to turn in Hannah's stressed-out mind.

CHAPTER SEVENTEEN

Bodhi ran the hot water until it came up to temperature then washed his hands at the stainless steel sink. He'd double-gloved to examine Jason Durbin, but an arterial wound was always messy. This one, particularly so. The bullet had severed the man's femoral artery in the inguinal region where it branched down from his groin and thigh. He'd probably bled out well before the news of the shot made it to the 9-1-1 operator.

He dried his hands carefully then waited for Chief Clark to come out of the ladies room across the hall. She emerged pale but dry eyed. She'd watched the autopsy wordlessly, her lips pressed into a thin line behind the clear visor.

"Let's go. We don't want to keep the Wonder Twins waiting," she said with a resigned sigh.

They took the wide stairs from the hospital basement up to the cafeteria where they'd arranged to meet up with Agents Thurman and Clausen. The police chief glanced at him twice as they mounted the staircase but looked away quickly, as if she couldn't quite make up her mind about asking him a question.

"It would have been quick."

"Pardon?"

"Jason Durbin would have bled out quickly. He didn't suffer long."

She blinked at him. "How did you guess—?"

"It's what any compassionate person would want to know."

She fell silent for a moment. Then, in a quiet voice, she asked, "Is it true—it would have been that fast?"

"I wouldn't lie about it. It's true. Probably a matter of seconds, not minutes."

It was true. A direct hit to an artery was a quick way to die. He thought of Sasha McCandless, a friend from home, who'd been knifed in her brachial artery. She was considerably smaller than Jason Durbin. If he hadn't been present when she'd been stabbed, she wouldn't have survived. Of course, if he hadn't been present she wouldn't have *been* stabbed in the first place—but that was a separate issue.

The femoral artery was the second largest artery in

the body, second only to the aorta. And unlike Sasha, whose artery had been cut but not severed, Jason Durbin's had been completely detached when the bullet tore through his lower abdomen.

"Okay. Thanks." She gave him a tremulous smile.

He pushed open the swinging doors and they walked into the quiet cafeteria. It was nearly two in the afternoon. The lunch rush had come and gone. Only a few tables were occupied. Their occupants sat hunched over cups of coffee whispering to one another in the hushed tones that became automatic in hospitals.

He spotted Clausen and Thurman at a rectangular table near the window and waved. Clausen nodded a greeting. Thurman twisted around and grinned.

He followed Chief Clark through the line. She selected a bag of chips and a slice of pizza that was being kept nominally warm under a heat lamp. He chose a clear plastic cup of nuts, a container of olives from the salad bar, and an apple. From the refrigerated case near the cashier lanes, she got a paper carton of milk. He filled a courtesy cup with water from the dispenser on the counter.

The cashier waved them through. "No charge, chief."

Chief Clark smiled wanly. "Thanks, Sandra."

They joined the NCSC agents at the table. Bodhi

draped the dead Chinese man's bag over the back of his chair.

Clausen skipped the small talk. "Did you finish the autopsy?"

"Yes. The cause of death was rapid exsanguination as the result of a wound to the common femoral artery."

"He bled out?" Thurman asked as he dipped a french fry into a pool of ketchup then popped it into his mouth.

Chief Clark and Clausen both averted their eyes from the pool of red on Thurman's plate.

"In broad strokes, yes. There's something called the triad of death. So, technically, it wasn't just blood loss. It's the combination of hypothermia, acidosis, and coagulopathy."

"Sure, okay." Thurman kept mowing down ketchup-drenched french fries while he spoke.

Bodhi speared an olive and turned the conversation away from blood. "One finding that might be of interest to law enforcement was the mud on his boots. There were lima bean seeds stuck to his soles."

"Did he grow lima beans?" Clausen asked, turning to the police chief.

"Not as far as I know. But, as I told Dr. King, Mark Olson leases a couple acres to a lima bean farmer." Chief Clark's voice was low.

"Olson? Does this mean you've changed your opinion as to whether Durbin started the fire?"

"No."

Clausen raised an eyebrow. "I see."

There was a lengthy pause, but the chief didn't elaborate. She focused instead on eating her pizza, crust first, which struck Bodhi as an unusual technique. But live and let live.

Thurman finally broke the silence. "Speaking of the Durbin-Olson situation, have you spoken to that attorney Mr. Olson retained?"

"No, I've been busy watching Dr. King hack apart Mr. Durbin and remove all his organs."

Thurman winced.

Bodhi put down his apple and reached for the bag hanging over the back of his chair. "Not to the change the subject, but I'm going to change the subject. Just as a reminder, we have two dead men down in the basement. This bag belonged to the John Doe I found in the meadow."

Chief Clark pursed her lips. "But it's empty."

"True. But last night I was assigned to clean out the basement at The Prairie Center—"

"Wait. They dole out punishments?" Thurman asked.

"It wasn't a punishment. It was a task that I was supposed to perform in a mindful way."

"Same difference."

"I was in the root cellar and I found a wheeled foot locker—something like a travel trunk."

"Aren't those usually locked?"

"Yes."

"But this one wasn't?" Clausen's eyebrow went up again.

"It's not now."

Clausen's lips quirked up, just the hint of a smile.

He loosened the drawstring and placed the knife and journal on the table. "Inside the trunk, I found clothes that would have fit the deceased and toiletries—all with labels and identifying information removed. I also found this knife and the notebook."

Chief Clark reached for the weapon. Clausen reached for the diary.

"This is a sharp blade, good quality. Too bad he didn't have this on him when he was garroted," the police chief mused as she examined the knife. "He might have stood a fighting chance."

She sheathed it and returned it to the table.

"The journal is encrypted. Agent Clausen is apparently a good code breaker." Bodhi explained for the police chief's benefit.

Clausen raised her head from the book. "I'm not bad. Can I hang on to this for a while?"

Bodhi looked at Chief Clark, who shrugged and said, "Sure. Just keep us apprised."

"But this means this guy was a spy—I mean, right?" Bodhi asked.

"Probably. And it probably means Fyodorovych offed him." Thurman's voice was matter-of-fact.

"What do you base that on?"

"The garrote. And the fact that he's almost certainly freelancing for his old employer."

Bodhi shook his head. "Can you fill me in? On the non-classified parts, at least? Because this story doesn't hang together for me."

Thurman took a breath and looked at Clausen. She closed the diary and pushed her half-eaten bowl of soup to the side.

Then she leaned across the table and said, "This is not to be repeated. If it is repeated, we'll deny having told you. And you'll both be on the radar of the Director of National Intelligence, which is not a place where you want to be. Are we clear?"

Chief Clark rolled her eyes over the top of her milk container but said, "Crystal."

"Sure," Bodhi agreed.

"Good. So, the short version is Russia and China

have both been trying to get their hands on Supra Seed's R & D for years."

"And by research and development, you mean corn seed?" Bodhi clarified.

"Right."

"How can it be top secret? It's growing all over the county and probably the rest of the state, too."

"And Nebraska and Iowa," Chief Clark confirmed. "But Supra Seed keeps a tight lid on its experimental seeds. The agricultural stores have lists of which farmers have been contracted to plant which specific lines of seeds. And if you're not on the list, you don't get the seeds."

"It's like a controlled substance," Bodhi marveled.

"It's big business. And it's serious stuff. Supra Seed's competitors would love to get their hands on those seeds to reverse engineer the gene lines."

"How?"

"By planting them under controlled conditions. The Chinese and Russians want to plant them, too. Because they have mouths to feed."

Thurman interjected. "Here's some background that will shed some light on the urgency of their need. In the 1930s, a guy named Henry A. Wallace was the United States Secretary of Agriculture."

"He later became FDR's running mate and was Vice

President for Roosevelt's first term. He was something of a controversial guy, so he only served one term. He went on to serve as the Secretary of Commerce," Chief Clark added.

They all looked at her.

"History major," she said with a shrug.

"Anyway, Wallace instituted the ever-normal granary, which functioned as a federal reserve for grain. His idea was to always keep production high. In boom years, the government would buy the excess, to keep prices from dropping. And in lean years, the government could release reserves."

"Okay, sure." Bodhi vaguely remembered the concept from some long-ago economics course.

"It was brilliant, for a while. Farmers loved it. But in the 1950s, Ezra Benson became the Secretary of Agriculture. Benson thought the grain reserve program was socialism. He wanted to compete with Russian and Chinese communist farms by glutting the international market with corn to depress prices. And instead of reserving the surplus, his idea is to use it as foreign aid to allies," Thurman continued.

"Ever since the 1970s, the government's been selling loads of corn to both China and Russia. They seemed to think it was humanitarian in nature, but we were making them dependent on us for food," Clausen added.

"And if they rely on us, we can control them by threatening to take it away," Bodhi understood now.

"Exactly. So, logically, they want to do an end run. They need to figure out how to grow corn with massive yields themselves."

"So ... they send spies here to do what? Steal corn kernels from the fields?"

"Maybe. Probably." Clausen nodded. "But they need more than the seeds. They need access to the scientific data. When to plant? When to water? How much? Which pesticides to use? When to spray? When to harvest?"

Bodhi thought back to his conversation with Hannah Lee Lin. "Isn't that all computerized? Couldn't they hack into the software programs remotely?"

Clausen chuckled mirthlessly. "If it were *our* software, maybe. But Supra Seed's stuff is locked down tight. The farmers who use their crop management software need key fob tokens to log in. A fob generates a single-use password each time the farmer logs into the system. And they're geographically limited—they won't work off the farm. Sort of like those grocery carts at some urban stores—the wheels lock up if someone tries to take them off the property."

"So—" Bodhi began.

"So, they must have an inside man, one or both of

the Russians or the Chinese must've turned a Supra Seed employee. Someone who has access to the data from the company side."

"Have you shared this theory with Supra Seed?" Chief Clark asked.

"Yes. They insist their people are all clean. But the security team is monitoring everyone who has access to the information that the Russians and the Chinese would want to get their hands on." Clausen patted the journal. "And if this book did belong to the Chinese John Doe, it looks like he did manage to get his hands on something. I'll just need to break the code to figure out what."

"Do you think he hid that trunk in the basement or do you think it was Fyodorovych?" Thurman asked. He directed the question toward Bodhi.

"The Russian. The monks said they'd asked the dead man to store his bag in the barn because it was made of animal hide. That's where I found it. Presumably, Gavriil Fyodorovych knew that's where he kept it and after he killed him, he took it. He would have had access to the basement."

"So, he'll be coming back for it." The police chief's voice was heavy. "Just what I need, a break-in at the monks' house. I've already got this fire and Jason Durbin's murder to deal with."

Clausen and Thurman exchanged glances. "We can keep an eye on The Prairie Center for you."

"Have at it."

Bodhi coughed. "You'll need to talk to Roshi Matsuo and Bhikkhu Sanjeev."

Another look passed between the federal agents. Bodhi fixed his gaze meaningfully on the encrypted journal.

After a moment, Clausen sighed. "Fine."

CHAPTER EIGHTEEN

Thursday evening

The conversation between Clausen and Thurman and Sanjeev and Matsuo had gone about as well as a conversation between a pair of NCSC agents and a pair of Buddhist monks could reasonably be expected to go. The agents wanted to search the farmhouse from top to bottom and interview all the silent retreat attendees, novice monks, and assorted others present. The monks bemusedly rebuffed that request but permitted the agents to stake out the property from the vantage point of the barn.

Bodhi, having autopsied two men in two days, welcomed his evening work assignment of washing and drying dishes. It was restorative and productive, rather than reductive. He was drying the big metal stockpot when Matsuo came into the kitchen. Bodhi kept his focus on the shiny pot until Matsuo touched his sleeve.

"Yes?"

"May I talk to you when you finish? Tonight, Bhikkhu Sanjeev will lead the Dharma discussion. If you're willing to miss it, I thought we could discuss your meditative progress."

Bodhi returned the pot to its designated shelf and hung the damp dish towel over the oven handle to dry.

"Roshi, I'm afraid I haven't made much progress during this retreat." Surely the Zen teacher knew as much. Bodhi had spent more time in the morgue than on his meditation pillow.

Matsuo smiled his slow smile. "I see. But you did come here for a reason, yes? And the reason was not to solve murders."

"That's true." Bodhi searched for the right words. "I came here because I needed to figure something out."

Matsuo sat on the wooden bench along the wall near the back door and gestured for Bodhi to join him. "And have you figured it out?"

Bodhi sat. "No."

"Do you no longer have the need to resolve it?"

"I haven't had time."

"Ah, but you have had time. You just chose not to use it in silent meditation."

"The Buddha says not to harm any living creature."

"This is true."

"Someone is harming people. One of your neighbors has been killed, and one of your students—or a guest, at least. I have training that can help the police to stop the killing. If I don't do that work, I'm not following the Buddha's precept. I'm allowing harm to come to living beings."

Bodhi had worked through his position on this matter months earlier, when he'd been asked to consult on a death cluster in Florida.

Matsuo considered the proposition with a serious expression. Finally, he said, "You may be right. There are followers of the Buddha who believe activism, for lack of a better word, is in keeping with the teachings. I'm not sure I agree."

"Why?"

The monk exhaled slowly. "It's true that we should stop violence and killing when we can. But the trick is to do it without anger. That's a difficult task—to do it with compassion. This Gavriil person has killed at least once before, perhaps more?"

"Almost certainly more."

"If you encounter him and he wishes to kill you, what will you do?"

"I ... what should I do?" This question had stymied him more than once.

He was perhaps unusual for a practicing Buddhist in that, so far, people had tried to kill him on two separate occasions. The first time, he had refused to defend himself, and his friend Sasha had nearly died as a result. The second time, just a week ago in Canada, he had taken steps to protect Eliza—and himself. He wasn't sure which path was the right path.

Matsuo smiled serenely. "I believe that you must stop him. If that means he must be killed, then it must be done lovingly."

"Kill him lovingly?"

"Yes. Assuming a killer cannot be stopped any other way, then a surgical killing, done without anger or right-eousness, may be the correct thing to do. You would be protecting innocents, and you would be doing him a kindness because allowing him to continue killing will be to doom him to bad karma."

Bodhi blinked at this calm defense of taking a life. "I don't think I could do that."

Matsuo shrugged. "It is not the Theravada way. Sanjeev would disagree with me. He'd say we don't know all the facts—what if this Chinese man had worse karma than Gavriil? Then his killing was good karma.

You see? It's an endless loop. He would say the right path is to focus on your own enlightenment."

He'd never heard any teacher—neither Theravadan nor Mayahanan—express the views Matsuo held. They felt alien to him. And very wrong, viscerally wrong. The monk was watching his face.

"I think I need to meditate on this, Roshi."

"I see. But, that's only half the answer."

Typical Zen master, Bodhi thought as he smothered a grin. "Oh?"

"Yes. The great difficulty is in taking a stand without anger."

Just then the kitchen door opened, and Feng came in from the backyard. He drew up short when he saw Matsuo and Bodhi sitting on the bench. He smoothed out his startled expression and bowed his head.

"Roshi, I didn't mean to interrupt."

"It's no matter, Feng. Have a peaceful evening."

The novice bobbed his head again. Then he slipped off his shoes, lined them up squarely in the rack by the door, and walked through the kitchen into the front of the house. No doubt he was going to join the Dharma talk in progress.

Matsuo watched him leave. Bodhi thought he saw a shadow in the monk's eyes as he tracked Feng's movements.

"Take, for instance, Feng," Matsuo said in a quiet voice.

"What about him?"

"Feng burns with a righteous anger. He believes that some of our neighbors are violating the *bija niyama,* the germinal order, which is the law of physical organic things."

"From a rice seed, only rice."

"Yes, and from a corn seed, only corn."

He tilted his head. "He objects to the GMOs?"

"He takes issue with all the hybrid lines of corn. The ones hybridized for sweetness, for yield, for pesticide-resistance. It offends him, as if it is a perversion. He protests, he educates about sustainable organic farming, he makes his voice heard in the community. This is all good. But he does so in anger. That's bad karma for him —not the seed company, not the farmers. Do you see?"

Actually, he did see. In his experience, it was rare to leave a conversation with a Zen teacher with a sense of greater clarity. But in this case, it had happened.

"Yes, I do. Thank you for talking with me."

Matsuo beamed at him. "Thanks for talking with me, friend." He stood and walked gracefully toward the front of the house. "May you be happy, well, and find peace, Bodhi."

CHAPTER NINETEEN

ette rocked back in the wooden rocking chair on her deck and tilted her head up. Her nightly vodka tonic sat on the small side table at her elbow. The Pleiades star cluster was especially bright tonight.

She found six of the Seven Sisters easily thanks to a clear night and plenty of experience gazing up at the sky and focusing on the cozy group the sisters formed together. Then she spotted shy Pleione, the mother, hiding behind her brighter, bolder husband Atlas. Only Asterope evaded detection.

She'd find the dim star. It was a matter of perseverance and patience.

She glanced away, sipped her drink, and looked back, found Maia again and allowed her eyes to shift up and left. She looked away again then back—and *there*—she made out the faint gleam of Asterope.

Gotcha!

She smiled up at the shimmery light then took another drink of her cocktail.

After a moment, she laughed softly, thinking of her own sisters. Growing up in a town much like this one, they'd spent too many nights to count lying on their backs studying the constellations overhead. Telling each other stories about the Seven Sisters, based loosely on Greek mythology, as the stars sparkled above them. Trading secret wishes and fears. Weaving big dreams of fantasy futures.

Now one sister lived in a tasteful flat in Paris, married to an international banker; she spent her days drinking good coffee and painting vivid images on big canvases in a studio overlooking the Seine.

The other sister had a place in the Pacific Northwest, perched on rugged, beautiful landscape on the edge of a cliff overlooking the ocean, a rugged, handsome husband, and a pack of barefoot, tangle-haired children who climbed apples trees and looked up at their own night sky.

And she had at least one murderer, at least one arsonist, and some unknown quantity of international spies running around her corner of the world.

On a happier night, she would also count her blessings: Her quiet deck; the view of the sun rising over golden fields as far as the eye could see; and friendly, honest citizens she'd sworn to protect and serve. But this was not a happy night.

She drained her glass and closed her eyes as the sharp burn of alcohol swam down her throat to her belly.

She looked back up at the Pleiades. Someone had told her once that Native American farmers called the constellation the Seeds because it resembled a heap of seeds. They also used it as a planting calendar. When the star cluster became visible in the pre-dawn sky in June, the Native Americans planted the last of their seeds, and when it was visible in the fall's morning sky, they harvested their plants. All without the benefit of crop management software, geolocated one-time passwords, deadly pesticides, or specialized corn lines kept under lock and key.

She laughed again, bitterly this time, and her thoughts turned from girlhood dreams and traditional farming cultures to Jason Durbin and Mark Olson.

Despite the lima bean seeds stuck to the bottoms of Jason's boots, she didn't believe he'd set fire to Mark's field on Wednesday morning. If he'd tromped through the leased lima bean field on Monday evening when he confronted Mark about the pesticide, those seeds could have been clinging to his soles all week.

But she didn't think so. The lima bean farmer said the Durbins didn't make a habit of cutting through his field to reach Olson's place. And she'd seen the proof of that herself. Dolly, Jason's wife, had walked the long way around, following the drainage ditch along the road frontage, when she'd brought over coffee and water for the firefighters.

Aside from it being country commonsense not to trespass on another man's land in a county where chickens outnumbered people and guns outnumbered chickens, Jason would have had his own reasons for not walking through his neighbors' fields. They all sprayed. He didn't. He was committed to organic farming and dead set against using chemicals on his crops. He wouldn't have risked tracking something back and contaminating his own land. That was just business sense. Principled, yes. But also pragmatic.

The same combination of principle and pragmatism also meant there was no way on the Lord's great green earth that Jason Durbin would set fire to fields that were within a quarter mile of his own land. Everyone in rural Illinois knew how fast a field could burn. The risk to the Durbins' farm had been real during that blaze. In fact, the only reason Jason hadn't put on his volunteer firefighter gear and joined the effort at Mark's was because he'd been standing guard over his own crops with a hose in hand.

Aided just a bit by the vodka, which she'd poured with a more generous than usual hand, she voiced her conviction out loud in the dark. "Jason didn't set that fire."

But someone had. Olson's attorney had hammered that point home more than once in their brief call. There was an arsonist in Onatah.

Of course, there was also a killer.

Her thoughts turned to Mark Olson. The lima bean farmer said that Mark *did* cut across the fields he leased to get to the Durbin farm. Which was fair, he owned them after all. Mark had confronted Jason, to accuse him of setting the fire—he admitted as much. But he'd cooled down fast. Mark wasn't the hothead of that pair; that had been Jason.

And, from a purely logical standpoint, Mark lived to the west of Jason. He wouldn't have walked right past Jason's property to the abandoned homestead to the east of Jason's to shoot him, which was where the shot had come from.

No, Mark was a hard-nosed sonofabitch, but he wasn't an assassin. He was a businessman, calculating and always acting in his financial self-interest. He'd probably been busy getting his papers together to file an insurance claim for the fire when Jason had been shot.

"Mark didn't kill anybody." Her words rang out in the still night again.

An owl stirred, hooted in protest, and flew out of her big oak tree.

She needed to find the woman who called in the shooting. She needed to talk to the farmers planning to file the class action lawsuit against Supra Seed. She needed ... to sleep.

She looked up one last time to say good night to the Seven Sisters in the sky then turned and went inside. She snicked the lock into place, put her glass in the sink, and trudged upstairs to collapse into bed.

CHAPTER TWENTY

Hannah checked the deadbolt. It was locked, just as it had been when she'd checked it twenty minutes earlier.

Calm down, she ordered herself.

But as the darkness had gathered outside her window, her nerves had slowly ratcheted up. She'd grown more anxious with each passing hour.

Now it was midnight. The witching hour.

Twenty-four hours had passed since she'd nearly died—and a farmer named Durbin *had* died, she reminded herself.

When she'd first read the article on her computer, she'd steeled herself to talk to the police chief. But then she'd seen Bodhi King's picture. A seed of hope had bloomed, and she'd decided to speak to him instead. Maybe it was stupid to base her decision on one brief interaction, but she felt as if she knew him. She could trust him to help her see her way through this mess.

The decision made, she'd pulled on her shoes hours ago, while it was still daylight, fading—but not yet dark. She'd hurried down the stairs to her car in the attached garage accessible from the basement, the keys jangling in her hand.

But she'd stopped three-quarters of the way down and gripped the steel handrail, overcome with doubt.

She couldn't just show up at The Prairie Center. What if *he* was still there? She didn't expect him to be— he would have contacted her by now if he'd seen her office blinds set at the prearranged height. A signal. *I need to talk. I left you a note.*

He'd never ignored the signal before. So he must have left—must have been recalled to Beijing by the Ministry of State Security. She imagined the missive: *You and your American contact have done well. We have what we need. Come back now. No, don't contact her. It's for her safety, and yours.*

Surely that's what had happened. Surely there was no harm in her knocking on the wide front door of The Prairie Center and asking the kindly monk who answered if she could see Bodhi King.

But what if she was wrong. If he was still there. If

she somehow blew his cover, and her own. It was too great a risk.

She'd turned and jogged back up the stairs, run into her apartment, and slammed the door behind her. Had secured the lock and deadbolt. And had paced while her worry grew to a frenzy.

She had to think of a way to see Bodhi without showing her face at The Prairie Center. But how? Her ability to problem solve was clouded by fear. Frozen, even.

She reminded herself she was a scientist. A woman of reason and fact. She would get the sleep that had eluded her last night and wake refreshed. Then she could form a plan.

All she needed to do right now was to quiet the primordial part of her brain that was silently screaming messages about danger and darkness.

She took several slow, deep breaths. Tried to chase out the boogeymen with fresh oxygen. Her heart slowed, but only marginally.

So she stood in the center of her small, spare apartment and worked through her *Wushu talou,* the unarmed fighting forms she knew by heart.

She wished for a weapon—her sword or spear or staff —but she had none. She'd paused her training when she'd moved to Illinois.

Instead, she kicked and punched and stretched, again and again and again, until she was slick with sweat and her muscles trembled with fatigue.

Then she washed her face, brushed her teeth, and checked the lock one final time. She collapsed into bed. And, finally, she slept.

CHAPTER TWENTY-ONE

Bodhi was surprised to see Feng sitting in the dark and quiet parlor when he turned out the kitchen lights to go upstairs to bed. It was very late, after midnight. Which was perhaps only somewhat late for most adults—but not for adults who would be awoken by a singing bowl at five a.m.

The monk sat in the alcove that protruded from the westward-facing side of the house. A window seat was built into the space, and a bay window with three angled panes of glass was set into the dark wood wall. During the day, it made an inviting spot to read.

Feng was not reading. He sat with his back against the front window and his feet pointing toward the back window. His knees were pulled up near his chest and his arms were wrapped around his shins. It was a protective, almost furtive posture. He was staring out into the night.

When Bodhi padded into the dark room on bare feet, Feng flicked his eyes away from the window for no more than a half-second to glance at Bodhi. Then he went right back to looking outside.

"Are you okay?"

Bodhi crossed the room to the alcove.

Feng kept his eyes glued on the window. "I think so."

His voice held a note of uncertainty. Bodhi hesitated. He would have asked to join the man on the window seat, but the only spot available would be impeding Feng's view of ... whatever it was he was looking at.

Bodhi tried to track his gaze. He seemed to be staring toward—but not at—the barn. "Are you waiting for someone?"

At the question, he snapped his eyes away and locked them on Bodhi. "No. Are you?"

"No. But you seem to be looking for someone or something specific."

Feng frowned and gestured toward the window. "When I was watering the garden earlier while you and Roshi Matsuo were in the kitchen, I thought I saw movement near the trees. It could have been a deer or fox, but, I thought we should be very cautious—considering what happened to our Chinese guest. So I walked up the path to the barn just to check, and I know I heard an engine in the woods behind the shed."

He heard Thurman and Clausen moving their car into the barn.

"Did you see anything?"

He shook his head. "No. I thought perhaps someone had gotten in and taken the tractor, but the shed was locked up tight."

Bodhi felt his brow wrinkle, and he smoothed it. "That's good. But, Feng, a man was murdered in the field. I don't think it's safe to go wandering alone back there after dark."

The worry in Feng's eyes dissipated and a fire took its place. He held Bodhi's gaze. "Fear is just misplaced attachment."

"Okay. Good night." He dropped a hand briefly on the man's shoulder then turned to go.

Bodhi left him sitting there, watching the barn from which Clausen and Thurman were watching the house.

CHAPTER TWENTY-TWO

It was after midnight.

Gavriil sat under a starry, moonless sky on the same stump where he'd left the garrote days earlier. Aside from the yellow police tape draped across the stump—which he'd simply pushed out of his way— there was no hint that he'd killed a man here. No blood, no signs of struggle. Of course, San hadn't had time to react. Gavriil had come up behind him like a cat.

He would have preferred to stake out the doctor from the barn he'd moved into on the other side of the organic farm. He felt safer there now, but he needed to be close enough to move on the doctor when the federal agents hiding in the barn left.

He'd watched through his binoculars as the dark sedan had arrived on the property. The two law enforcement agents and the doctor climbed out of the car and walked together through the front doors of The Prairie Center. The doctor wore San's knapsack on his back.

Eighteen minutes later the agents exited through the same doors. No doctor. He'd watched them get back into their sedan and drive down the long driveway to the road. He kept his attention trained on the house.

Four minutes later the car reappeared on a dirt path that wound through The Prairie Center's property. For a moment, he was confused. Then he realized they must have taken an access road—a relic left over from an earlier incarnation of the farm. He'd slipped behind a tree to watch from a concealed position.

The car bumped slowly through the woods, then out into the clearing, and came to rest behind the barn. The male agent got out of the car then ran up and opened the wide back doors into the barn. The female agent guided the car inside. Her partner ran through behind the sedan then pulled the doors shut.

From the time the sedan emerged out of the wooded section of the farm, the entire operation took a minute, maybe a minute and a half. The smoothness and speed with which they feigned leaving the property and then managed to secrete themselves away inside the barn displayed practiced teamwork, good communication, and competence. Gavriil was impressed and more than a little worried.

He stayed in the trees while the monk called Feng left his work in the garden to come investigate.

Some sound or blur of motion must have caught the monk's attention. He followed the footpath from the garden to the barn then detoured away from the barn on a diagonal to check the door to a large shed set several yards away from the barn. He yanked on the padlock that secured the shed door. It held.

Check the barn, Gavriil urged silently.

Feng did not check the barn. He skirted to the left and returned to the house.

Gavriil returned to his stump. He'd been sitting on the rough, uneven stub of an oak tree for hours now. He checked his watch—four hours. Two hundred and forty minutes. There'd been no movement from within the barn in all that time. Nobody slipped out and into the woods to relieve himself or herself. Nobody got tired and called it a day. Nobody sneezed or passed gas loudly.

He sat, silent and patient, and watched the barn while the agents inside the barn sat, equally silent and infinitely patient, and watched the house.

Finally, at two o'clock in the morning, Gavriil powered on his cell phone and sent a text to a cell phone number registered to a restaurant in Kyrgyzstan:

Needed: Backup for an operation on behalf of our mutual former employer. Will pay market rate + 12.5 %.

Need someone versed in wet work, fluent in English. Will pay premium for someone with decrypting experiencing and familiarity with Chinese language. Qualified candidate will have physical ability and mental willingness to perform wet work.

He scanned over the help wanted ad and gave a satisfied nod. Then he powered his phone off again so as to prevent anyone from triangulating his location using cell phone tower registration.

He looked up at the stars bunched up overhead and wondered what their names were. His work hadn't left much time for hobbies, but he'd always imagined he'd retire someday to a house on a high peak where he could build a powerful telescope and spend his nights on a virtual journey throughout the galaxy.

If he saw this mission through to completion, he would finally have the funds to make his retirement dream a reality. He just needed a hired killer or two to lend him a hand.

CHAPTER TWENTY-THREE

Friday morning

Feng was already—or still—awake when Bodhi wandered down from the second floor. He had lit the candles and was preparing to strike the standing bell to wake the others.

"Did you sleep well?" he asked, the wooden block poised above the lip of the bowl-shaped, inverted bell. The bell rested on a fat round pillow.

Bodhi considered the question. "Under the circumstances, I'd say so. And you?"

Feng glanced at the bay window, an involuntary but telling gesture. Then he shrugged. "Well enough, I suppose. I need to run outside for a moment. Would you strike the bell to wake the house and signal the beginning of noble silence?"

"Of course."

Feng handed him the block and hurried into the kitchen. Bodhi watched through the doorway while the monk pulled on his shoes and removed a jacket from a hook set into the wall near the door. He grabbed the small basket and the gardening shears and unlocked the kitchen door.

Bodhi resisted the urge to caution him to stay in the garden. The man was an adult, after all. And if he was being honest, he didn't want to give Feng any ideas.

He tapped the stick hard against the bell and listened as one long note filled the air. Some people hit the bell as he had, and others preferred to run their sticks around the outside of a bell's rim, which caused a continuous vibration. Bodhi had always preferred to strike the bell. He raised the stick and hit the bell a second time just as the ringing from the first strike faded into nothingness.

Operating under the near certainty that he'd once again miss most—if not all—of the day's meditation sessions, he lowered himself to the bare floor beside the bell to take advantage of the silence. He could squeeze in a short mindfulness practice before Feng returned or any of the others came downstairs.

He cleared his mind, closed his eyes, and centered his attention on his breath.

He wasn't sure how long he sat—it could have been three minutes or it could have been thirty. But when he heard the door to the kitchen opening, he opened his eyes and stood.

He walked out to the kitchen.

Feng was filling a tea kettle. "I picked some fresh rosemary and mint for tea, if you'd like to join me."

"Thank you."

While Feng prepared the tea, Bodhi swept the floor. They worked in companionable silence. The only sounds were the roiling and bubbling of the water, working its way up to a boil, and the *swish, swish, swish* of the broom's bristles, brushing across the floorboards.

Bodhi finished his task and returned the broom to the tall, narrow closet built into the wall. Feng took mugs down from the cabinet and arranged a tray. Bodhi picked up the woven doormat in front of the kitchen door and stepped outside to shake out the debris trapped in its weave-mostly clods of dirt and grass, a few pebbles.

He waved the mat up and down, over the porch railing, letting the wind help do the job. A clump of mud fell to the porch at his feet. He draped the mat over the railing and stooped to pick up the mud. As he stood to pitch it into the dirt underneath the porch, something caught his eye. The lump was dotted with cream-colored, slightly flattened seeds, ranging in size from one-third to three-quarters of an inch.

Lima bean seeds.

He picked them out of the earth, brushing the loose mud off with his fingertips. He pocketed four of the seeds and one hard, rock-like nugget of mud. Then he retrieved the doormat and went inside.

"The tea's ready." Feng gestured toward the small, scarred wooden table against the wall where he'd laid out the tea tray.

Bodhi replaced the mat and washed his hands at the sink. He joined Feng at the table.

"Thank you."

Feng nodded. "Of course."

"You're in charge of the garden?"

"Mother Nature's in charge of the garden, but I help her out. I enjoy working with my hands. The smell of fresh dirt and green shoots is my favorite perfume." He smiled.

"Were you a gardener, before?" Bodhi knew the novice would understand that he was asking about his life before he took up his robes.

Feng laughed. "No. I was an insurance adjuster in Sacramento. I didn't have a houseplant, let alone a garden."

"That's a big change."

Feng sipped his tea. "It's been a good change. Aside from having the opportunity to learn so much here at the center, this place suits me."

"Onatah?"

"Yes. I like the pace, the feeling of community among the farmers, and the simpler relationship between a man and his food. It feels as if this is the way it's meant to be. Picking dinner from the garden, not from the Whole Foods salad bar."

Bodhi didn't doubt the man's sincerity. But the idyllic, bucolic picture he painted didn't square with everything Clark, Clausen, and Thurman had told him about big business, agri-technology and world domination.

This wasn't the time to engage him in a philosophical discussion about designer seed lines and drop management software, though. Bodhi had actual questions that needed answering.

"Do you grow lima beans here?"

Feng furrowed his forehead. "No. Maybe in a few years. I'm hoping to clear a plot for the three sisters. Why do you ask?"

"The three sisters?"

"That's what the Iroquois called corn, beans, and squash. Most, maybe all, of the Native American tribes grew them together and used them together in cooking. The three plants grow best when planted together because they're interdependent and they provide complete nutrition. All from one plot."

"How does that work? The interdependence, I mean?"

"The corn is tall. And the beans—usually lima beans or pole beans—need something to climb as they grow. So the cornstalks fit the bill. The corn supports the growing beans. Then the beans do something called nitrogen fixation. Do you know what that is?"

"I haven't a clue," Bodhi admitted.

Feng was warming to his subject now. He leaned across the table, his eyes bright. "There's a bacterium that colonizes the roots of bean plants and pulls nitrogen from the air, converting it to ammonia in the soil. This fertilizes the soil for all three plants. It's brilliant."

"And the squash?"

"Squash is a sprawling plant with big leaves. So the squash leaves keep the soil moist and cool, shading it from the sun and preventing weed growth. And squash have prickly stems. So animals avoid the plants."

Bodhi nodded, impressed. The three sisters appeared to have the perfect mutually beneficial arrangement. "It sounds as if they'd be worth planting that way. Do many of the farmers still use the system?"

Feng's face clouded. "No. Even the organic farmers are obsessed with yield, yield, yield. Corn is king around here. Beans and squash would take up valuable inches of soil. They want to plant 'fencerow to fencerow,' as they like to say. Bigger is always better. And of course the company farmers would laugh themselves silly at the thought of trading their chemicals, genetic marvels, and computerized watering systems for Native American companion planting methods that are hundreds of years old, maybe even older."

Feng's voice was laced with bitterness and something more—despair, anger? Bodhi couldn't tell. Before he could respond, the monk stood.

"I've enjoyed talking with you. I need to go prepare for my day."

"I enjoyed it, too. Thank you for the tea and for explaining about the three sisters. I hope you have a peaceful day."

Feng met his eyes. For a moment, Bodhi thought he was going to share something important—a secret dream or fear, perhaps. But the moment passed. Feng's expression closed off. He nodded, took the tea tray to the sink, and left the room.

Bodhi felt around in his pocket and removed a lima bean seed. He balanced it in his palm and looked down at it.

CHAPTER TWENTY-FOUR

"I don't have time to talk to you about lima beans, Dr. King." Elise Clausen's voice was polite, but her strained patience was clear.

Agent Thurman clasped a hand on Bodhi's shoulder. "Don't mind her. She was up all night trying to break that code."

Thurman was unnaturally cheerful for a man who'd spent the night in a barn. Especially considering he'd had Clausen for company.

"Can you answer my question, then?"

Thurman tapped a finger against his lips. "You want to know who around here grows lima beans, right?"

"Not exactly. I'm looking for a list of farmers—or even home gardeners—who grow three sisters companion gardens."

"And the three sisters are corn, beans, and squash, correct?"

"Right."

Thurman lifted his shoulders then dropped them in an exaggerated shrug. "I wouldn't know. They wouldn't be on our radar unless hostile foreign governments are trying to hack into their computers to access their gardening plans. But, I'm pretty sure those plans are freely accessible at every hipster co-op and vegetarian potluck in the country."

"And on the internet. And in readily available gardening magazines. And fourth grade textbooks," Clausen added without lifting her eyes from the diary.

"Not exactly breakthroughs in modern science you're talking about," Thurman concluded.

Bodhi exhaled. "There were lima bean seeds on the bottoms of Jason Durbin's shoes," he reminded them.

"Right, and leaving Chief Clark's belief that Durbin wouldn't trespass aside, he did live next door to a lima bean farmer."

Thurman airily dismissed the only piece of actionable evidence Bodhi had found during the autopsy as if it was no great shakes. Which, Bodhi was willing to concede, it may not have been. But it was the only shakes they had, as it were.

Bodhi was about to remind the agents of this not

insignificant fact, but the man door to the barn opened and Chief Clark hurried inside, stamping the dirt off her boots.

"Morning," she said crisply.

"She might know," Thurman said to Bodhi. "Morning, Chief."

Clausen looked up and nodded a greeting to the police chief.

"What might I know?"

"Who around here maintains a three sisters garden," Bodhi said.

She pulled a face. "I'd have to think about it. But right now, we've got a bigger issue to deal with."

"Not another dead body?" Bodhi asked, steeling himself for her response.

"No, not yet, at least. But I just walked through my crime scene—"

"Which one?" Thurman countered. "There are three of them, after all."

"This one, Agent Thurman. The meadow where Dr. King found your Chinese spy."

"And?"

"And someone spent a fair amount of time there. Last night, if I had to guess. The grass was disturbed, and so was my crime scene tape."

Clausen closed the journal. Thurman's happy-go-lucky grin slid off his face.

"Fyodorovych?" Clausen asked.

"It's almost got to be, doesn't it?"

Bodhi interjected. "One of the monks thought he saw someone or something moving in the trees last night. Then he said he heard an engine running in the woods, so I assumed it was you two circling back to the barn."

"The car was us, most likely us, but Thurman stayed in the car until we were in the clearing," Clausen said.

"That Russian SOB was watching us?" Thurman marveled, half-impressed, half-outraged. "Take me to the spot," he said to Chief Clark.

"What about your partner?"

"She's not going to be any use until she cracks that code. She can stay here with Dr. King. We won't be long."

Thurman pulled on his jacket and followed Chief Clark out the door.

Bodhi watched Clausen work. Her blond head was bent over the encrypted book. Scraps of paper covered the workbench she'd commandeered as her makeshift desk. When she stopped scribbling on the scraps, she chewed on her pencil, holding it sideways between her teeth.

After about a minute, she must have felt him studying her. She raised her head and blinked at him.

"What?"

"Sorry, I didn't mean to break your concentration. You're very focused."

Her lips curved into a smile. "Focused, hmm? I think you're being polite. Charlie would say you mean intense. Or single-minded. Or relentless."

"None of those is a bad trait."

"Not for a man. But for a woman ..." she trailed off.

Bodhi wasn't in the business of psychoanalyzing federal intelligence agents. He said nothing.

"Spit it out," she demanded.

"Spit what out?"

"You've got something to say. You look like you're going to burst."

"I don't know you, but you do come across as sort of ..."

"Dour and humorless?"

"Uh, serious. I'd say serious."

She blew a stray tendril of hair out of her face. "I'm a conventionally attractive single woman working as a federal law enforcement agent. I have certain limitations on my ability to be winning, charming, or funny. Charlie

Thurman, lacking such constraints, is well-loved by everyone he meets. And as his partner, I instantly become the foil. The Felix Unger to Oscar Madison; the Bert to his Ernie. You get the idea."

Picturing Agent Elise Clausen as a bright yellow puppet did him in, and he chuckled at the image before quickly regaining his composure in response to Clausen's glare.

"Sorry," he said. "I made the mistake of visualizing you as Bert. Anyway, are you making any progress?" He gestured toward the book.

She sighed. "First, I thought it was a substitution cipher, but that's not feasible."

"Why?"

"Well, for one thing, there's not a Chinese alphabet. Written Chinese is a logosyllabic language. The characters function similar to glyphs, and each syllable in a word is represented by one character. I've heard estimates that there are as many as fifty thousand characters."

"But the average Chinese person doesn't know that many," Bodhi pointed out.

"True, but still, if you were going to do a substitution cipher, first you'd want to transliterate the characters into one of the romanized writing systems, probably Pinyin. That's what the Japanese did in World War II.

They transliterated Japanese characters into a romanized system called Romaji, then used an alphabet keyboard to encode the syllables."

"So, it could be a substitution code."

"It could be, but assuming he wrote in columns bottom to top, right to left, my frequency analysis leads me to believe it's not. It just doesn't make sense. Even though the characters look columnar to me, I'm playing around with it as if he wrote it left to right, top to bottom, just to see. But that doesn't work either."

Bodhi thought. "Would Cantonese be transliterated the same way?"

"No, Pinyin is short for Hanyu Pinyin—it's the standard Chinese romanization system. But standard more or less means Mandarin, and you can imagine how Cantonese holdouts feel about that. Cantonese is transliterated into its own system called—wait for it—Cantonese Pinyin. Why?"

"I'm sure our dead spy was fluent in Mandarin, but Matsuo, the Zen teacher, also knows enough to have a conversation. He tried to talk to the man, and he said our guy answered him in what sounded like Cantonese. I'm sure he was feigning that he couldn't speak Mandarin, but if he could also speak Cantonese, maybe he used that system for his code?" Bodhi shrugged.

Clausen's face lit up, transformed with excitement. "That could be it. Thank you."

"I hope it helps and isn't just another dead end."

"If it doesn't work, at least I'll have ruled another option out."

"Great."

She smiled and reached for the pencil, eager to be finished with their conversation so she could return to her work. Then she paused for a moment and laid the pencil down.

"You helped me work through my problem, so I guess it's only fair to help you—what's the deal with the lima bean seeds?"

"Jason Durbin was pretty impassioned about sustainable agriculture, right?"

"That's putting it mildly."

"There's a monk at The Prairie Center who's also very interested in sustainable or traditional farming methods. He and I were the first people awake this morning. He tracked lima bean seeds into the house on his shoes, but he doesn't grow them in the garden."

"Okay, that's a little odd."

"That's what I thought. He told me all about the three sisters. And he's also the guy who thought he saw someone in the woods. He's on high alert. It's as if he's nervous about something."

"Maybe he's nervous because one man was murdered and another disappeared from the house. I'd be nervous if I were staying there. It's like living in a slasher film."

He had to concede that point. "That might explain some of his jumpiness, but something feels off."

"What?"

Bodhi shook his head. "I don't know, Agent Clausen. All I really know is Jason Durbin had seeds on his shoes that he shouldn't have. When I perform an autopsy, the police are typically fairly interested in evidence like that —someone else's hair on the victim's clothing, a match-book from a specific bar in the victim's purse, that sort of thing. I'm a pathologist, so this isn't my area of expertise, but it seems significant."

She tilted her head. The sunlight from the window behind her streamed in and framed her face with a luminous glow. "When you put it that way, you're right. I think the issue is you're not an expert in crime scene investigation, and none of us is an expert in plants." She gave a small laugh. "Too bad there's no such thing as a plant pathologist."

He stared at her.

"Get it, a plant pathologist? Someone who's an expert in plants and ... see, this is why I leave the jokes to Thurman."

"No, it's not a joke. I know one."

"You know one what?"

"A plant pathologist. She works at Supra Seed."

"Seriously?"

"Yes."

"What are you waiting for? Call her."

Bodhi hurried out of the barn. He turned in the doorway. "Thank you for talking it through with me. And good luck with the code."

She lifted her left hand and waved to let him know she'd heard him, but she was already concentrating on her cipher. He closed the man door quietly behind him and pulled out his cell phone as he walked toward the clearing.

CHAPTER TWENTY-FIVE

Hannah gripped the phone, pressing it to her ear, unable to believe her good fortune. She realized he was waiting for a response.

"Oh, yes. I remember you."

"I'm glad. I hope it's okay to call you at work?"

She glanced around the quiet laboratory. "Yes, of course."

"Good. I'll get right to the point. I need your help."

She blinked. Was this some sort of stress-induced aural hallucination? Or was this the actual answer to her literal prayers? Bodhi King needed *her* help? That solved the problem of crafting a way to see him for help with her problem.

"I'll be happy to help you if I can."

"I need to know everything you can tell me about some lima bean seeds."

"Lima bean seeds?" she repeated to make sure she'd heard him correctly.

"I know you work with corn, but I was hoping—"

"A seed is a seed. I can help you," she cut him off quickly before he had second thoughts and contacted some other lima bean seed expert. She needed to talk to him about a murder. If her entrée to that conversation was lima beans, that worked for her.

On the other end of the line, he exhaled. It was a barely audible *whoosh* of relief. "Fantastic. Thank you. So, this is somewhat time sensitive."

"A lima bean seed emergency?"

"Pretty much. And, as you might remember, I don't have a car here. Could you come to me?"

"Um, at The Prairie Center?" That was less than ideal, but at this point Hannah wasn't going to quibble about the details.

He hesitated. "Sort of. I know this may sound strange, but could you drive straight past the driveway and continue on another tenth of a mile or so? There's an access road that runs through the property. I'll meet you there. We need to go to the county hospital."

She had zero desire to set foot on The Prairie Center's property until she confirmed that Zhang had really left, if not the country, at least the county. How she planned to do that remained a mystery. But one step at a time. So she didn't question why he wouldn't just meet her at the end of the driveway if he was in such a hurry. If he wanted her to pick him up on the side of the road, that suited her just fine.

"No problem. Access road, got it. What time?"

"Like I said, it's time sensitive, but I realize you have a job and a schedule of your own, so how soon could you leave work?"

"I can leave right now. I'm not doing anything crucial at the moment."

That was true enough. She'd forced herself to come into the lab, but mainly she'd spent her morning alternately staring out the window and refreshing the news feed on her computer in a futile search for updates on the murder of Jason Durbin.

"Perfect. I'll owe you one," he promised with a smile in his voice.

Oh no, she thought. *You won't owe me anything, because I plan to collect right now. I'm going to tell you I'm the one who called 9-1-1 the night Jason Durbin was killed and you're going to keep me out of trouble.*

She hung up the phone, scooped up her purse and keys, and hurried out of the lab. Her supervisor was in meetings all day, so she told his assistant she was going to the university campus over in Golden Plains to do some research. She guessed she might be gone all afternoon. The assistant jotted it down and waved her away.

CHAPTER TWENTY-SIX

Gavriil palmed the steering wheel of the rental car, unable to believe his luck. The scientist was leading him straight to the doctor, which solved his primary problem that he couldn't be two places at once.

After the police chief had shown up at The Prairie Center, he'd slipped into the woods and back to his home base. He hadn't surveilled the scientist in a while, so he fetched the car from the shed where he'd hidden it and drove toward her workplace. He tried to minimize driving as much as possible since he had rented the car using one false identification, which he'd immediately dumped, and was driving it using a second one. Getting around this godforsaken hinterland required a vehicle, though. So he'd just have to obey the traffic regulations and hope for the best.

He'd set up on a hill behind the high school and trained his binoculars on her car in the Supra Seed employee parking lot. That was all the closer he dared to get to the corporate campus. The company's security team was serious business. All ex-military, ex-government, ex-law enforcement. He had no desire to get on their radar.

He'd been surprised to see her hurrying across the lot to her white car. It wasn't yet lunchtime. But he welcomed the action, so he set aside the binoculars and started his engine. He crawled down the steep hill at a pace that would ensure she'd pass him before the access road dumped him out on the main road. He saw her car coming around the bend and braked, waiting for her to zip by. Then he hit the gas and turned onto the county road.

He followed her at a comfortable distance. The road didn't intersect with anything other than private drives and farm access roads for another seven miles. He could let her get ahead without worrying that he would lose her.

Instead he worried about the silence from his contact in Kyrgyzstan. He'd expect some acknowledgment. A message that he was working on finding the talent Gavriil needed. Something. But he hadn't heard a peep.

There were too many players now. Eliminating the

Chinese agent hadn't made his job easier. Inexplicably, it had made it harder. He needed help. Now.

His fingers itched to text the man again, but this state's laws prohibited both the use of handheld devices and texting while driving. He'd studied the applicable local rules and regulations before taking on the assignment, as was his practice. He'd known too many good operatives who'd gone down on minor traffic violations.

Up ahead, the scientist blew right past The Prairie Center's driveway. Gavriil raised his eyebrows. He'd been so sure. Where the devil was she going then?

Ten seconds later, she slowed to a stop. She was stopping at the access road. The same road the federal agents had taken to get to their stakeout spot in the barn.

He dropped his speed and fell back.

A lone figure opened her passenger side door, ducked his head, and entered the vehicle.

From this distance, he couldn't see the man's face. But based on what he could make out—lanky frame, curly hair—Gavriil was certain it was the doctor.

Now he faced another decision.

The doctor wasn't carrying San's bag. Should he risk a trip to the monks' farmhouse, right under the noses of the police and federal agents to retrieve San's book—*his* book? He'd killed the man for it, after all. It belonged to him—to him and to Russia—now.

He hesitated.

No, follow the pair of civilians. He couldn't leave Onatah just yet. Not with so many loose ends. And he lacked the cryptography skills to decode the book. That task would require specialists—SVR agents, most likely —and it exceeded the scope of his mission. So what difference did it make if the book was out of his hands for a few more hours or even a day?

Once he had more boots on the ground, he would regain possession of the book. Either through theft, negotiation, subterfuge, or violence. The method made no difference to him.

The better course was to neutralize the human assets first.

He increased his speed and closed the distance between his car and the white sedan.

CHAPTER TWENTY-SEVEN

B ette and Agent Thurman returned to the barn shortly after Bodhi left to do whatever it was he planned to do with a plant pathologist and a handful of bean seeds. He'd tracked the two of them down in the clearing to tell them he was leaving, but Bette hadn't quite understood his plan.

Agent Clausen looked up from her code-breaking efforts when Bette pushed open the door. Thurman followed her in and closed the door behind him.

"Learn anything useful?" Clausen asked.

Bette let Thurman answer. Clausen was his partner, not hers.

"Just that Fyodorovych must have ice water running through his veins."

"Why's that?"

Thurman glanced at Bette before he answered. She nodded. She agreed with his assessment.

"He wasn't just watching the house. He was watching us, too."

Clausen's blue eyes widened. "He was watching the barn?"

"Yes, based on the pattern of the flattened grass, he rotated between two positions. One facing the farmhouse's doors and one facing the barn."

Clausen tapped her pencil against her teeth. The little clink of tooth enamel on wood made Bette cringe.

"He must have a pair of powerful binoculars."

"Deductible business expense," Thurman cracked.

Bette interjected. "What's the next move? I can put out an all-points-bulletin on this guy, but I need something to give the state troopers or it'll be a pretty useless APB. Do you have a recent photo? Make and model of his ride? Anything?"

The NCSC agents exchanged glances.

"Nothing," Thurman said.

Nothing we'll share with some local police department is what he means. Bette bit down on her lower lip to keep her thought unexpressed.

"So I think an APB would be premature at this juncture," Clausen added smoothly. "Any word from your fire inspector?"

She's trying to change the subject. But Bette realized she needed them more than they needed her right now, so she answered the question with a non-answer that would have made any federal agency proud.

"His investigation is ongoing, so I think it would be premature to discuss it at this juncture."

"Touché," Thurman said with an approving nod.

His partner iced him with a look. He glanced away first. Bette heard a buzzing sound. Clausen looked at her piles of papers then pawed through them until she dug out her mobile phone.

"Clausen."

The person on the other end began to speak immediately. From her spot by the door, Bette could hear a fast, clipped voice speaking, but not the words. Beside her, Thurman stood up a little straighter, as if he recognized either the voice or the urgency in the delivery or both.

Clausen's porcelain skin turned a shade lighter. She was almost translucent. Bette could see the blue-green veins in her neck. Her mouth opened and formed a small 'O.' She nodded wordlessly.

Finally, she cut off her caller. "Troy, I'm going to put you on the speaker. I want Charlie to hear this. The Chief of Police of Onatah is here with us. She needs to hear this, too."

A pause while Clausen listened.

Her mouth tightened. "I'd say she needs to know. This is her problem, too."

Another pause.

"Do what you need to do to CYA. I'm making the call, she hears it too." She jabbed a button on her phone and stepped closer to Bette and Thurman.

Troy, who needed to cover his ass for reasons unknown to Bette, spoke in a measured but serious voice. "Can you all hear me?"

"Loud and clear," Thurman confirmed.

"Yes," Bette said.

"I'll keep this brief. Agent Clausen can fill in the details later. Our team intercepted a text message sent at 12:18 a.m. Central Time. The text was destined for a cell phone registered to a restaurant/bar in Bishkek, Kyrgyzstan. The restaurant specializes in Russian dishes. The restauranteur specializes in Russian espionage for hire. The text originated in central Illinois. Before you ask, no we weren't able to triangulate it. Too much open space out there. The text read as follows: Needed: Backup for an operation on behalf of our mutual former employer. Will pay market rate + 12.5 %. Need someone versed in wet work, fluent in English. Will pay premium for someone with decrypting experience and familiarity with Chinese language. Qualified candidate will have physical ability and mental willingness to perform wet work."

After a beat, Thurman asked, "Can you send us the exact wording?"

"I'd rather not."

Clausen frowned. "Okay. Then repeat it."

She nodded to Thurman, who pressed a button on his own phone. Bette could see that he was recording. Troy repeated the text. Then Thurman turned off his recording app.

"Thanks, Troy," Clausen said.

"Did you pick up anything from Fyodorovych's phone?" Thurman asked, stowing his phone back in his pocket.

"It's a European model, off-brand. Probably a burner, although I imagine Fyodorovych won't ditch it until he gets an answer. Which he's not going to get, because it never reached Bishkek."

Clausen's face relaxed incrementally.

Bette cleared her throat. "I want to be sure about one thing. The message referenced 'wet work' twice. That's a euphemism for murder, correct?"

Thurman nodded. "The term originated with the KGB and was adopted by the CIA. Now, any assassin for hire is liable to use it, but in this case given the shared former employer reference ... it's not posturing."

"Got it." She nodded briskly and pretended her insides weren't twisting themselves into a tight knot.

"Thanks for the call, Troy. Sit on this for now," Clausen said.

"Wait. If we wanted to, do you have the ability to spoof the number in Bishkek and text a response?" Thurman asked.

Troy bristled. "Of course, I have the ability. But not if I'm sitting on this."

"Understood. Right now, just hang tight. But it's good to know we have it in our back pocket." Thurman's tone was appeasing.

"Will do. Listen—keep in mind that Fyodorovych is naked in there. Russia almost certainly hired him, but this is a contract job. He's not getting operational support from Moscow. He's a throwaway. You corner him, ... he'll do what it takes to survive." Troy's voice was strained.

"Your concern is duly noted, Agent Blackman." Clausen clicked her phone off.

They looked at each other for a long moment.

Bette spoke first. "It's clear he knows the encrypted journal isn't in the basement of the farmhouse anymore. And given that he spent the night watching the house, we should assume he knows Bodhi took it. Otherwise, why bother with the house?"

Thurman nodded his agreement. "And he's willing to kill for it. But I don't think he'd call in reinforcements just to kill a civilian doctor. He's obviously capable of doing so himself. He offed the Chinese agent."

"You think there are multiple targets?" Clausen asked.

"There must be."

"Who, though? I guess the Chinese contact, whoever that is," she answered her own question.

"And you two," Bette said.

"Us?" Thurman threw her a skeptical look.

"You said it yourself. He spent the night watching the house *and* the barn."

CHAPTER TWENTY-EIGHT

odhi directed Hannah to the hospital cafeteria and suggested she grab a snack or drink while he ran down to the morgue to fetch the seeds from the room where he'd performed Jason Durbin's autopsy. Durbin's body had already been sent to the funeral home, and Chief Clark planned to send one of her officers over to pick up his clothing and personal effects so his wife wouldn't need to do it.

The dirt from the bottom of the boots wasn't a personal effect, and it should have been stored as evidence. As an outsider, Bodhi didn't have access to an evidence storage locker, so the mud and seeds were currently stored in a clear plastic sandwich bag. He was pretty sure chain of custody would be a problem if the seeds ever ended up in a courtroom, but since nobody else seemed to view it as evidence, there wasn't much he could do about it. He grabbed the baggie, relocked the door with his temporary key card, and took the stairs back upstairs two at a time.

Hannah sat at a table near the back of the room, her hands cupped around a mug. Her head was turned. She gazed out the window. Even in profile, he could see the faraway look in her eyes.

"Is everything okay?" he asked as he dropped into the chair across from her.

He knew it wasn't. Although he'd only spoken to her once before today, he could see that she was preoccupied. She'd been quiet during the drive. And fidgety. But it wasn't his place to pry her concerns out of her. She'd talk if she wanted to talk to him.

"What? Oh, yes. Did you get what you needed?" She turned to face him with a too-bright smile.

"Yes. May I use your napkin?" He gestured toward the unbleached square.

She handed it to him. "Sure."

"Thanks."

He unfolded the napkin and laid it flat on the table, smoothing it with one hand. He removed a seed from the baggie then reached into his pocket and removed one of the seeds he'd found when he'd shaken out the doormat back at the farmhouse. He placed them side by side on the napkin: the one from Jason Durbin's boot on the left side of the napkin; the one from the floor on the right.

Her expression changed from one of distraction to one of sharp professional interest. She leaned forward.

"May I pick them up?"

"Yes. Please don't mix them up, though. I'm not sure it matters. But in case it does, let's keep track of which is which."

"Of course."

She reached for the one on her right, his left. She held it up to the light and turned it from side to side then bounced it in her palm. She returned it to the napkin. Picked up the other seed. Repeated the process. Then she replaced the second seed, the one from The Prairie Center, and leaned back in her chair. She looked at him for a moment with curiosity sparking in her clear brown eyes.

"Well?" he asked.

"Well, they're both lima bean seeds, but you already knew that. They're definitely from the same seed line. Based on their size, shape, and color, I'd say they're heirloom seeds—King of the Garden Pole. They're known for being producers, and they get really tall. Up to ten feet."

"You can tell all that from looking at it?"

She laughed. It was a warm laugh that, inexplicably, conjured thoughts of hot caramel.

"It's my job. I'd be a pretty terrible plant pathologist if I couldn't even identify a lima bean variety."

It was his turn to lean forward, excited. "Can you tell if they came from the same package or lot or whatever?"

"I could, if I took them back to my lab to analyze them. But just from eyeballing them, no."

He deflated, just a touch. Then he had another thought. "Could you tell if they were in the same soil, if I gave you soil samples?"

"Piece of cake. I'm good at that. You know how wine aficionados can tell you all about a wine without tasting, just by smelling it? I can do that with dirt."

"That's lucky. You wouldn't want to have to taste it to tell."

Another caramelly laugh.

He removed a clod of dirt from the bag and placed it beside the seed from the Durbin farm. He removed the clod of dirt from his pocket and placed it beside the other seed. She poked at each in turn. Then, as promised, she picked up first one and then the other and sniffed each of them. She put them back on the napkins then brushed her hands clean.

"What's the verdict?"

"Those are the same. It's good, rich soil. Lots of nitrogen, phosphorus, and potassium. Homemade fertilizer—wood ash, green sand, and I smell bananas, most likely from a compost bin."

"Do you know any farms that use that sort of soil?"

"And DIY vegetable and mineral fertilizer? Not a one. It wouldn't be cost-effective in a full-scale commercial farming enterprise."

"What about a small family farm? Or even a large garden?"

She thought. "Maybe your friends at The Prairie Center."

"But they don't grow lima beans. My guess is this farm or garden doesn't only grow lima beans. Probably plants a traditional three sisters garden."

She wrinkled her brow, but only for a moment. Then her face relaxed. "The Native Ways Traditional Community Garden is the most likely candidate. It's just what it sounds like—a community garden dedicated to using Native American and other traditional methods of gardening."

"Why would people out here need to have a community garden? Everyone has more land than I can even imagine."

"That's true, but it's more of a gardening experiment, I guess. I only know about it because they basically do the same thing I do, only not under controlled conditions and with diametrically opposite goals and methods. But they invited me to speak at a program they sponsored at the county library."

"How many people attended?"

"Oh, less than twenty. Sixteen, maybe. It could have been eighteen. The monk from The Prairie Center was there—the one who tends the garden."

"Feng."

"Yes, that's his name. Oh, and—" Her face fell.

"What is it?"

"Jason Durbin, the farmer who was just shot, he was there."

Bodhi's pulse ticked up. He didn't believe in coincidence. "When was this meeting?"

"Back in the spring, before planting season." She was staring down at her lap.

He could see she was twisting her hands around and around beneath the tabletop.

"Hannah, what's the matter?"

"It's about Mr. Durbin."

"What is it? Did you know him?" He was suddenly very grateful he hadn't taken her to the morgue itself. Although Jason Durbin's corpse was gone, his blood-soaked clothing wouldn't have been the most pleasant reminder.

"No. I mean, I knew who he was. And I knew he had a Crop-Clear claim. He said his neighbor's spray killed his harvest. He went to the town council and everything."

"Oh. I thought you might have been friends. You seem so upset."

She peered up at him from under lowered eyelids and took a deep breath. "We weren't friends, but I am upset about his death. I was there when he was murdered."

Bodhi guided Hannah out into the hallway by her elbow. Somehow, with one hand, he'd gathered up the seeds and dirt, deposited her mug in the bin set out for dirty dishes, and grabbed her purse off the back of her chair.

He piloted her along a short, tiled hallway to a set of steel doors, which he pushed open with his hip. The doors opened into a wide landing. The sign on the wall had a down arrow labeled 'Morgue' and an up arrow labeled 'Diagnostic Laboratory Services.'

He eased her away from the door then handed her bag to her.

"You were with Jason Durbin when he died?" he whispered.

"I wasn't with him. I was walking outside the fence." Her voice shook. This was her chance to tell him everything. Beg for understanding and ask him to help her with the police chief.

"It was you? You're the woman who called it in?"

She nodded.

"Why haven't you called back? Chief Clark needs more information—the investigation's stalled, Hannah." He furrowed his brow, confused.

"I know. I'm sorry ... I panicked. See, I wasn't just taking a walk. I was ..."

She stopped as the sound of shoes hitting metal rang out from the floor below. Seconds later, a young man in a white lab coat tripped up the stairs with a specimen carrier bag in his hands. She tried not to imagine what might be inside.

"Oh, Dr. King." The man stopped short. "I'm so glad I ran into you. The morgue supervisor asked me to find out what you want us to do with your John Doe's remains. Is he going to be staying with us for a while?"

She turned to see Bodhi frown at the man. "Is there a space issue?"

"No, we've got room for him. We just need to know if he needs negative temp."

"Ah, yes. We don't have any solid leads on his identity at the moment, but there's reason to believe he's a Chinese national. So, it could be a while. The freezer, for sure. A regular cold chamber won't do—he may start to decompose before we get his name. Thank you."

"No prob, Doc. I'll let the boss know." He nodded a goodbye and resumed his jog up the stairs, presumably to the laboratory wing.

Hannah pressed herself against the wall. She felt her knees buckle. She began to slide along the cinderblock.

"Hannah?"

She was hot but shivering. She shook her head to clear her thoughts. She searched his concerned face. Her stomach was churning, but she had to know.

"You have an unidentified corpse who's a Chinese national?" she said between chattering teeth.

"Yes. He was staying at The Prairie Center. I found him in the meadow behind the meditation maze on Tuesday morning. He'd been murdered." His voice was gentle.

She squeezed her eyes shut. "I can tell you his name. He was called Zhang San. And he's the reason I was out walking by Jason Durbin's farm when he was shot."

CHAPTER THIRTY

Bodhi's heart thudded in his chest. He was going to have to ask her to positively identify the body. There was no way around it. He'd help her through it, but it was necessary. He knew Chief Clark, Clausen, and Thurman would all want to witness the identification. And, frankly, Hannah looked like she was going to pass out or vomit. Waiting for them to arrive would give her a chance to come to grips with the news.

He kept one eye on her to confirm that she wasn't going to fall over while he dialed Chief Clark's cell phone number.

"Clark."

"Can you come to the morgue, STAT? Bring Clausen and Thurman."

"Are you safe? Is he there? Shit, I was just getting ready to call you." Her voice was stricken.

He blinked in confusion. "Yes, we're safe. Is who here? What's going on?"

"Fyodorovych called in reinforcements. The NCSC intercepted the message, so it wasn't delivered, but he's trying to hire assassins. We think to kill you. And probably Clausen and Thurman, tying up loose ends."

Bodhi's already racing heart started to beat double time. He breathed in for a long four count and out for seven.

That was better. His heart rate was still too fast, but the organ was no longer in danger of exploding.

"But if his message didn't get through, nobody's coming to kill me. I mean, right?"

Hannah's eyes snapped open as she heard his end of the conversation.

"Unless he gets impatient and decides to do it himself. We don't know where he is right now. We've been out searching every barn, garage, and shed. No trace of him yet."

"In that case, I think my issue still takes priority."

"It can't possibly. Does this have something to do with those blasted seeds?"

"What?" He'd forgotten about the lima beans. "No.

It has to do with your dead organic farmer and our John Doe."

"Both of them?"

"Yes. Ms. Lin was there when Jason Durbin was shot—"

"She's my female caller?"

"Yes, and she can identify John Doe. She knows him."

He hesitated, not wanting to say more in front of Hannah while she was in her current state. He didn't think she was in psychological shock, but finding out her secret boyfriend was a Chinese spy might just get her there.

"Are you being serious?"

"Entirely."

"We're on our way. Do not go outside. In fact, lock yourselves in the morgue. Don't open the door for anyone. That includes me—if it's safe to let me in, I'll say, um, Asterope. If I say Alcyone, don't let me in. It means Fyodorovych got to us. Repeat it."

"Asterope, good; Alcyone, bad. Do you think this password thing is really necessary?"

"I don't want to find out—do you?"

She had a point there. "Fair enough. But listen, I can't lock Hannah Lin in a room with a corpse, especially not that corpse. I'll find an empty office and text you the location."

He ended the call. Hannah was watching him.

"Did you get the gist of that?"

"Someone wants to kill you, it sounds like."

"Yes. Not just someone. The someone who we believe killed your ... friend. We need to find a safe spot."

"Wait. I have to explain something to you. I ... the reason I didn't come forward after Mr. Durbin was killed was that I was afraid. I didn't want people to find out about what I was doing with Zhang. I know you won't understand. I know it was wrong ... but I—"

"Hannah, shh. Please, it's okay. I know what you were doing, you don't have to explain yourself to me." He soothed her.

"You know?" She couldn't keep the shock out of her voice.

"Listen, I won't judge you. The fact that you were having an affair or a secret relationship or whatever you were doing isn't my business. And right now, it really isn't important. Right now, we need to lock ourselves in an office and wait for the authorities. Okay?"

She stared down at her feet.

He lifted her chin with his finger. "Hannah, look at me. It doesn't matter."

"You think ... I wasn't ..." She trailed off.

He watched her face, waiting.

She opened her mouth. Didn't speak. Shut it. Finally, she shook her head. "Thank you for understanding."

He smiled. "No thanks needed. Now, come on—we need to get out of this stairway."

CHAPTER THIRTY-ONE

G avriil was getting antsy. The doctor and the scientist had been in the hospital for over an hour. He'd spent that time sitting on a bench near the patient drop-off and pick-up that seemed to be where the not fully mobile population of the county waited for their rides upon departure.

He assumed these easily winded, slow shuffling bench sitters were all receiving outpatient treatments because American television had taught him that patients being discharged from hospital stays were wheeled out in wheelchairs as a matter of policy.

This detail didn't matter to him but it gave him something to ponder while he waited for the pair to finish their business and leave. He wondered what business they had. If the doctor had made the connection between San and his asset, he expected the federal agents would make an appearance soon.

No more than three minutes after he had the thought, the agents' sedan rolled into the parking lot. He watched from behind the magazine the kind lady with the oxygen machine had left behind when her daughter-in-law picked her up.

The male agent was driving today. Gavriil wondered if the pair switched back and forth every other day or if it depended on where they were going or if they had a passenger or some other variable.

The man didn't park in the visitors' lot. He drove right up to the circular patient loading area and stopped the car six feet away from Gavriil's bench—maybe fewer.

Gavriil rarely experienced an adrenaline rush these days, unless he was killing someone. But at the moment, his blood was rushing in his ears and his mouth was drier than vermouth. He willed himself to sit still. No tapping toes, jittering leg, or drumming fingers. No outward sign of nerves.

The female agent and the police chief jumped out of the car and hurried through the doors into the hospital. His thigh muscles twitched, desperate for his brain to send the signal to leap up and follow, but his brain stayed cool.

He stared at his magazine, reading an extensive

product review of a countertop yogurt maker for the home cook. After a moment, the car pulled away, circled the parking lot, and disappeared from view.

Had he merely dropped them off? Or was he going right now to get backup to arrest San's collaborator?

Gavriil supposed it didn't matter. One way or another, they'd be coming through that door again. And he was ready.

He checked the weapon on his hip. It was loaded. The silencer was in his pocket. He'd timed himself under all sorts of field conditions. He could screw a suppressor into place in less than a tenth of a second.

The four targets would exit the building, possibly to be picked up by the fifth. Gavriil would stand, drop the homemaker magazine, click the silencer onto the end of his gun, and mow them down with a series of muffled pops. Not silent, but definitely suppressed.

He flipped the page to a recipe for cheeseburger casserole.

An hour passed. Fifteen minutes more. His legs were getting stiff and numb. It wouldn't do if his feet fell asleep. Shooting multiple people while hopping around as the sensation of pins and needles ran up his legs was not the plan.

He stood. Stretched. Decided to do a quick lap around the perimeter of the building. It was best practices, anyway. You never knew what you were going to find.

What he found was the black sedan parked at one of the hearse bays at the morgue's loading dock. The man must have circled the building and come in through the delivery entrance. Now there were two exits to cover and two cars to watch.

His plan to massacre them as they walked out the door crumbled around him. It was probably for the best anyway. Shooting someone literally at the emergency room door was a good way to improve their chances of survival.

Patience. You'll have your chance, he told himself.

He ran around the side of the building and got into his rental car, moving it to the gas station across the street. From his new vantage point, he could see both the scientist's white car and the agents' black one. Then it was just a matter of following their two-car convoy when it inevitably passed him on the highway.

CHAPTER THIRTY-TWO

The new plan wasn't much of a plan, Bette thought to herself. She sat behind the wheel of Clausen and Thurman's car, which was parked sideways across the driveway to The Prairie Center, and waited for Bodhi. He'd gone inside to gather his belongings and say goodbye to a bunch of folks who presumably couldn't even respond.

But she did agree with Thurman's assessment that The Prairie Center was too exposed. There were too many ways to approach by vehicle—by driving straight up the driveway or by looping around on the access road or, with enough gumption, by careening through the woods. There were too many ways to approach on foot— provided the approacher didn't have any qualms about trespassing, which she imagined described Fyodorovych accurately.

Her house was a fortress. And not by accident. Bodhi'd be safe there. He'd have to bunk with Thurman. And Clausen and the Supra Seed scientist could share the other guest room. Bette wasn't giving up her king bed for anyone.

Why Clausen had insisted on wrapping Hannah Lee Lin into their protective cocoon remained a bit unclear to Bette. She'd told them everything she knew when she identified the garroted man's body—which wasn't much.

His name was Zhang San. He was in the country visiting universities to decide on a post-doctoral program in engineering. He'd arrived in town a few weeks earlier, just passing through, and they'd spotted each other at the library and had bonded. He'd decided to extend his visit.

This was all entirely believable. The last census had put the county's Asian population at 0.02%. Bette half-suspected that Hannah made up one hundred percent of that 0.02%. Seeing someone who looked like her, in the general sense, would have been a rare treat.

Hannah's story about San included nothing that indicated she knew he was a spy. Nothing that indicated she was romantically involved with the man, although she'd implied as much. After a quick pow-wow with the NCSC agents, Bette and Thurman had agreed Hannah most likely been an unwitting mark. Maybe San had rifled through her notes from work or had broken into her computer, but she seemed unaware of any breaches. Only Clausen seemed skeptical about Hannah's story.

At least she'd given Clausen and Thurman a name.

She'd given Bette a big, fat nothing. When Bette had questioned her about Jason Durbin's shooting, she'd gotten tearful right away.

She insisted she'd just been out walking.

Going to meet San, Bette had asked.

Not exactly, had been the answer. There was no prearranged trust. She hadn't heard from him in several days; she was worried. She wanted to check on him.

He had no cell phone and she didn't want to call The Prairie Center—he was embarrassed about his English, although she claimed he could speak the language, and the monks discouraged calls to the house phone, anyway.

She'd decided to walk to The Prairie House instead of driving because it was a pleasant night. She'd spent the day cooped up in the laboratory. The fresh air would do her good.

The rest was exactly what she'd said when she called the emergency dispatch—Durbin had yelled, a shot had been fired, she had run.

She told Bette she didn't know the farmer had been hit. She hadn't heard anything after the shot. She'd panicked and had run all the way home. She hadn't brought her cell phone with her because it was dead. Which was why when she got home, she called through her computer. She wasn't trying to mask her identity. She was sorry she didn't respond to the public request for her to call back, but she didn't know anything more.

The story more or less hung together, but it didn't help Bette one bit. Maybe it was a good thing Clausen had insisted on driving Hannah's car back to her apartment to get her things and then bringing her to Bette's house. Bette could take another crack at her.

She peered through the windshield, scanning the horizon, while Bodhi finished up inside.

"Please come back for a visit when you can do the work," Sanjeev said from the doorway of Bodhi's shared dormitory room.

Bodhi turned from the bed, where he was rolling his clothes to repack them. He heard disapproval in the monk's words but he knew if he mentioned it, Sanjeev would claim that any judgment Bodhi felt came from himself. So he let it go.

"I'd like that."

Sanjeev watched him for another moment. Then he

said, "Matsuo tells me he mentioned Feng's sustainable farming group to you last night."

Bodhi cocked his head and searched the teacher's face, trying to make sense of the non sequitur. "Yes, *bhante*, he did."

"They have good intentions."

"Of course."

Sanjeev smiled at him. "Be well, Bodhi King."

"Be well."

Bodhi had already said goodbye to Matsuo, so he zipped then shouldered his backpack, smoothed the bed linens, and walked out of the bedroom. He was halfway down the stairs when Matsuo's words from the previous night came back to him: *Feng burns with a righteous anger.* A burning anger directed mainly toward hybrid crops.

It was a basic tenet of Buddhist teaching that the lesson is in what is left unsaid as much as in what is said.

When he reached the bottom of the stairs, Bodhi swerved off his course toward the front door and detoured to the kitchen. He plucked the big ring of keys from the hook by the door then hurried toward the front of the house. The keys jangled against one another.

He raced down the porch stairs toward the driveway, gesturing for Bette to get out of the car.

"What is it?" she called as she walked toward him.

"I've been enlightened, I think. Leave your car blocking the drive and come with me to the shed, please."

She arched an eyebrow but strode through the long grass to meet him. "What's going on, Bodhi?"

"I'm checking out a hunch. I want a witness. And there's no better witness than the chief of police."

She fell into step beside him, and they hurried across the lawn to the shed. Bodhi flipped through the keys until he found the one that fit the padlock that secured the shed doors.

He turned the key and pulled down hard on the body of the padlock. The U-shaped shackle swung free. He removed the lock and pulled the doors open. His nose began to burn before he even stepped inside. The smell of something similar to diesel fuel, but sweeter, filled his nostrils.

Beside him, Chief Clark sniffed. "Kerosene."

"It's an accelerant."

Her eyes widened. "And that Crop-Clear stuff is highly inflammable. Supra Seed requires the farmers who use it to sign a statement promising to store it separately from gasoline, kerosene, and paint thinner. But you don't think ..."

"I do think. Feng's a member of some traditional

community gardening group and he's also a vocal opponent of GMOs and industrial farming."

"Sure. He's not the only one. But there's a pretty big leap from raising objections at a council meeting and setting a field ablaze."

Bodhi was silent for a moment. Then he said, "It's a religious mandate for Feng, though. He believes farmers like Mark Olson are violating one of the laws of the natural order set forth by the Buddha."

"And a Buddhist would destroy property over that belief?"

"Not typically. But, I'm pretty sure this one did. He was nervous last night. I thought he was watching the barn, but he must've been watching the shed. He knew people were lurking around the property. He may have been worried someone would come in here and find out what he's been up to."

It was Chief Clark's turn to fall silent.

Then she sighed. "Mark said when he confronted Jason about the fire, Jason denied involvement. Mark pressed him about that gardening group—Jason was a member, too. Mark's lawyer told me Jason claimed he had left the group over a disagreement but wouldn't say anything further. Do you think Feng would kill over his beliefs? If Jason knew what Feng had done and opposed it—would Feng kill him to keep him quiet?"

No, never, Bodhi's soul screamed. *You don't know*, his brain cautioned.

He stared at the containers of kerosene stacked neatly on the floor. He thought about how Jason and Feng had both had the same seeds on their shoes. They'd likely been together shortly before Jason's death.

After what felt like a very long pause, Bodhi shook his head slightly. "I don't know."

CHAPTER THIRTY-THREE

Hannah fidgeted in the back seat of her own car. She wished the five of them hadn't split up at The Prairie Center. She didn't know these National Counterintelligence and Security Center agents, and they made her nervous.

Part of it was right there in the name—counterintelligence and security—and part of it was because the female agent, Elise Clausen, had listened to Hannah's story with a frosty look.

The man, at least, had been kind. Charlie Thurman had consoled her on Zhang's murder and thanked her for finally coming forward about the night of the shooting at the Durbin farm. She wasn't as comfortable with him as she would have been with Chief Clark and Bodhi, but at least he'd extended her some human kindness.

But still. All things considered, she'd rather be back at The Prairie Center with Chief Clark and Bodhi.

Agent Thurman met her eyes in the rearview mirror and gave her an encouraging smile. "What do you do at Supra Seed, exactly?"

His tone was conversational, but Hannah really didn't feel like chatting. "I'm a plant pathologist. I work on creating disease-resistant plant lines."

The partners exchanged glances. Hannah bit her lip. "Nothing exciting—not like your jobs," she added. "What exactly do you do?"

"That's classified, ma'am."

Of course it was.

"Can you tell me why she has to drive my car? Or is that classified, too?" Hannah regretted her snarky attitude as soon as she'd said the words. It was one of her worst personality traits—when she was nervous, she could be mean. And she was very, very nervous.

Although she'd directed the question to Agent Thurman, Agent Clausen answered.

"Because I'm trained to execute evasive driving maneuvers at high speeds. Are you?" she snapped.

Hannah felt she'd earned the dressing down.

"No, I'm not."

After a moment, Agent Thurman tried to ease the tension in the car. "Chief Clark says her property has some of the best stargazing in the county. It's so dark, she can see the Milky Way most nights."

He made this announcement with the infectious enthusiasm of a puppy. Hannah half-expected him to bounce in his seat.

"That sounds cool. I grew up in San Diego. There was a lot of light pollution." Hannah smiled at Agent Thurman.

"Where did you go to college?" Agent Clausen asked.

It was a casual question, but everything about Agent Clausen made Hannah feel as if she were being interrogated.

She answered stiffly. "Berkley, for undergrad. I did my graduate work at the University of Chicago."

Agent Clausen made a *hmm* sound.

Agent Thurman said, "You must be really smart."

"I'm a hard worker. Oh, that's the turn off—right up ahead on the left."

Agent Clausen flicked the indicator light, which seemed to be the opposite of evasive driving to Hannah, but then she guessed they weren't currently being followed.

Were they?

She twisted around and looked through the back window. Nope. They weren't being followed. Not unless the would-be assassin had hijacked a tanker truck full of milk.

———

G avriil trailed behind the milk truck. He'd been using it as cover for miles now. It was obvious from their route that the two agents and the scientist were going to her apartment, having left the police chief and the doctor back at The Prairie Center. But for what purpose?

He shrugged to himself. Until he knew when his reinforcements would arrive, the best thing he could do was keep eyes on the targets. Steal the encrypted book if he could. Kill any or all of them if the need arose.

But there had been no word from Kyrgyzstan. That was beyond unusual. It had been twelve hours and counting. That realization made the hairs on his arms stand up.

Something was wrong. He glanced to his right at the cell phone charging beside him. He jerked the wheel to the right and swerved onto the shoulder of the road.

He picked up the phone and stared down at it. After a moment, he turned it over and popped out the battery. He pushed the button to buzz down the passenger side window. Then he checked the road—no traffic coming in either direction. He leaned across the seat and tossed the battery into the weeds growing alongside the berm. He removed the international SIM card and stowed it in his pocket. He'd dispose of that elsewhere. The phone itself would go in the trash at the gas station when he bought its replacement.

He hadn't survived eight years in the SVR and another six freelancing by disregarding the gut-wrenching moments when a person knows before he knows that something's not right.

He signaled to turn left and eased back onto the highway. The dairy tanker was just a pinpoint now. But it was of no concern. He knew where the white car was headed. In fact, he might as well stop at the Go-Now Market and pick up the new phone now.

The federal agents must be providing the scientist with an escort home. They'd probably search her apartment and tell her it was all clear. Their car was still at The Prairie Center, so eventually the police chief and the doctor would drive right by the Go-Now Market to pick them up.

He could wait in the parking lot. He'd use the time to set up his new phone and send a new text to his contact in Bishkek. It was safer than driving back and forth with a forged driver's license in his wallet, an unlicensed handgun in his glove box, and an illegal silencer and a stolen rifle in his trunk.

He executed a U-turn and headed back the way he'd come, cursing Americans and their love affair with driving.

CHAPTER THIRTY-FOUR

Friday evening

Thurman leaned on the Chief Clark's doorbell, a stack of pizza boxes in his arms. Clausen held a six-pack of beer. Hannah carried an overnight bag and wore an apprehensive expression.

Bodhi opened the door and hurried them into Chief Clark's front hallway.

"The kitchen's straight back."

Thurman and Clausen headed for the kitchen. Bodhi searched Hannah's face. "How are you holding up?"

"This morning I was analyzing a supersweet corn line for fungal sensitivity. Now I'm hunkered down in a safe house with two federal agents, the chief of police, and a forensic pathologist hiding from a murderous

Russian spy. In between, I identified a corpse. So to be honest, not so well."

There wasn't much to say to that. But everyone wants to know they've been heard, so he tried.

"I know it's difficult. And I'm sure seeing your friend in that condition was upsetting."

She nodded mutely.

"You're safe here. And I do know how a day can go sideways on you. I just found out that a monk I know set that big fire at Mark Olson's farm."

"Intentionally?"

"Yes."

She let out a small hiss of breath. "Does Supra Seed know?"

"Yes. After Chief Clark called for an officer to take him to the county jail to be processed, she talked to your company's security team."

"Was it Feng? The guy from the gardening group?"

"Yes."

Bodhi's heart was heavy. Feng had confessed right away. He'd told Chief Clark that as a former insurance adjuster he knew which accelerant would start the fire quickly and help it spread widely. She'd advised him of his *Miranda* rights, but he'd wanted to talk.

"I'm sorry." Hannah put a hand on his arm.

"Thank you. Let's eat before the pizza gets cold."

They joined the others around Chief Clark's solid oak table.

"That one's got vegan cheese," Clausen said, pointing with her beer bottle. "After Thurman and I checked out of our motel rooms, we had to go all the way over to the college to find a vegan pizza, so I hope it's good."

"Beer?" Thurman offered.

"None for me." Bodhi took a plate and a slice of pizza.

Hannah accepted a bottle and took the seat next to the chief.

They ate quickly and with little conversation. After the meal, Thurman and Chief Clark went outside to move all three vehicles—his, hers, and Hannah's—into the big barn out back. There was no need to advertise that the chief had company.

While Hannah took her bag to the room she'd be sharing with Clausen, Bodhi and Clausen cleared the table and loaded the dishwasher.

"I'm telling her about San. She needs to know. Do you want to be there to make sure I don't say anything classified?" he said to Clausen in a low voice.

She turned from the sink. "You don't know anything classified. But I don't think you should tell her."

"Agent—"

"I'm not sure if you're thinking with your big head or your little head, but she's not telling us everything she knows."

Bodhi felt his temper rising, recognized his anger, and then acknowledged that he was attracted to Hannah. He paused to search his conscience. No, he wanted to tell her because her friend had been murdered because he was a spy. She deserved to know the truth.

Clausen was watching him.

He gave her a level look. "I'm not going to lie to her by omission. Your partner agrees with me, by the way."

She shrugged. "Suit yourself. I warned you."

Footsteps sounded in the hallway then Hannah appeared in the doorway. "Do you two need any help?"

"We're finished. If anyone needs me, I'll be in the chief's study. She said I could work on breaking the code in there." Clausen filled the dishwasher with detergent and started the cycle then left the room.

"I don't think she likes me," Hannah said.

"She's just not a very warm person," Bodhi answered.

Hannah smiled. "Not very warm? More like frozen."

"Can we talk for a minute?"

Her smile wobbled. "Sure. But, what code is she trying to break?"

"That's what I want to talk to you about."

She pulled her shoulders back as if she expected a blow. "Okay."

"There's no easy way to say this. Zhang San was a spy."

She said nothing, just watched his face with big eyes.

"He was working for the Chinese government. The NCSC believes he was trying to reverse engineer the makeup of Maize46 and how to best grow it. I'm sorry, Hannah. He was probably using you."

She shook her head. "No. That's not right. He wasn't."

Bodhi paused. Of course he was. But he let the comment pass unchallenged.

"Gavriil Fyodorovych was working on behalf of the Russian government in an effort to get the same information. He killed your friend to get his hands on a diary or journal that was written in code. I found it in the basement of the monk's farmhouse."

"You have it?"

"Yes. Agent Clausen is an expert in manual decryption. She's trying to find out what it says. But that's why we have to be so careful. Fyodorovych is willing to kill for that book. And he knows we have it. And we have to assume he knows you had a connection with Zhang San."

Hannah closed her eyes and sagged against the wall.

CHAPTER THIRTY-FIVE

H annah couldn't face Bodhi anymore.

Correction, she told herself, *she couldn't face her own lies anymore.*

So she mumbled something about finding a book to read and escaped into the study. Too late, she remembered Agent Clausen was working at Chief Clark's desk.

The agent was staring down at Zhang's notebook, concentrating so fiercely that she seemed not to have noticed the door open. Hannah hesitated in the doorway, unsure what to do.

Without looking up, Clausen said, "Can I help you?"

"Oh, um, I'm sorry. I just wanted to get something to read ... I forgot you were working in here. I don't want to disturb you," Hannah said to the top of Clausen's wheat-colored head.

"Too late."

A wave of irritation stirred inside Hannah. "Why don't you like me? What have I done to you?"

Clausen put down her pencil and marked her place with her finger. Her pale blue eyes seemed to see right through Hannah.

"Since we're not in seventh grade, I'm not dignifying your first question with an answer, Ms. Lin. As to the second, it's not what you've done to me. It's what you haven't done."

"I have no idea what you're talking about."

"Really? So you've been completely forthcoming about your Chinese friend?"

Hannah's cheeks blazed. "Bodhi just told me you think he was a Chinese intelligence agent."

"I think that because he was one. And I don't believe that you're as innocent as you pretend to be."

Hannah's heart jumped in her chest. "I'm not sure what you mean."

"Well, for starters, anyone who knows even the most rudimentary Mandarin knows that Zhang San isn't anyone's name."

Clausen's eyes drilled into her. Hannah tried to speak but her throat was dry. She coughed and tried again.

"It is so."

"It's a placeholder name, Ms. Lin. It's the Chinese equivalent of 'John Doe.'"

"You know Mandarin?"

"I know enough to know that's not a real name."

Hannah exhaled. What the woman said was true, but what she was about to say also true.

"I swear to you, that's the name he gave me. It's the only name I know him by."

Clausen searched her face. Hannah tried to keep her expression neutral and wondered if Clausen found what she was looking for.

The agent returned her attention to her work. Hannah stood there feeling stupid.

After a moment, Clausen looked up again.

She waved a hand at the bookcases. "Well, go ahead and pick out some reading material."

Hannah walked over to the shelves, trying not to make any noise.

She kept her eyes on the spines of Chief Clark's book collection and asked, "Do you need any help with the code? I mean ... I do know some Chinese. If you want ..."

"No thanks."

Hannah nodded and grabbed a memoir at random.

She craved Agent Clausen's approval, which was pathetic. She didn't know the woman. She also wanted to see herself as a good person. She tried to be a good person. But, deep in her heart, she knew she wasn't.

She fled with her book before Agent Clausen could see the tears shining in her eyes.

CHAPTER THIRTY-SIX

B ette and Bodhi sat on the back porch. He was looking up at the stars. She was staring down into her vodka tonic.

The door banged open and Hannah stepped outside, her arms wrapped tight around her torso. She stared up at the sky.

"Wow," she breathed.

Bette smiled. "Yeah." She loved introducing people to her naked-eye observatory.

Tonight, the deep purple sky was a riot of stars. The moon was the faintest sliver.

After a long moment of open-mouthed awe, Hannah dragged her eyes away and looked around the porch.

"Where's Agent Thurman?"

"He got a phone call. I think he's taking it in the dining room."

Just then, Clausen's pale, tense face appeared in the glass set in the door. She rapped on the window and gestured for them to come into the house.

Bodhi stifled a yawn as he stood. "What time is it?"

"Almost ten," Bette told him. She was tired, too. All this sitting around and waiting to be killed was exhausting.

They trooped inside behind Hannah.

Thurman was standing behind his partner. His usually relaxed smile was missing. A muscle in his cheek twitched.

Uh-oh, Bette thought.

"There've been some developments," Clausen said.

"Let's go sit in the living room," Bette suggested.

They filed wordlessly into her casual living room. It was her favorite room. Cream-colored fabrics, rich tan and gold accent pillows, the fireplace and mantle, the sconces on the wall. If the backyard was her paradise, the living room was her sanctuary.

Thurman, Bodhi, and Hannah arranged themselves on her couch. Clausen stood in front of the hearth. Bette took one of the wingback chairs.

"So this is a good news, bad news situation. The good news is I cracked San's code."

"Really?" Hannah asked.

"Really." Clausen gave her a long look. "Your friend

was pretty smart about it. I won't bore you with all the details but he used a romanized alphabet with a substitution cipher and the old four-corners method of converting Chinese characters into numerals. It's going to take me a while to actually decode his journal, but now it's just a matter of time."

"I'll put some coffee on," Bette joked.

"That would be great," Clausen said, dead serious.

"But not because Agent Clausen is going to be pulling an all-nighter deciphering a dead man's journal," Thurman said.

"What's going on?" Bodhi asked.

"That's the bad news. Gavriil must have gotten suspicious when his contact didn't respond. He dumped his phone and got a new one. Our office intercepted another text to the restaurant owner in Kyrgyzstan. He's still looking for a couple of paid assassins."

"That's not surprising."

"No, it's not. But this time the message was slightly different. In addition to the job posting, for lack of a better description, he wrote asking about the rules of engagement for taking out HUMINT," Thurman finished grimly.

Bette grimaced.

"What's HUMINT?" Bodhi asked.

"It's short for human intelligence. An asset. A mole.

He's asking if he can kill Zhang's contact," Clausen explained.

Hannah blanched. Then she lifted her chin. "Funny he's asking now. He already tried to kill me once. Your dead organic farmer was collateral damage."

Bette watched the others' expressions. Clausen's was knowing. Bodhi and Thurman both looked stunned. Bodhi's eyes were wide. Thurman's mouth hung open.

Bette shook her head. She'd known that girl had been holding out on her.

She rose. "I better go see about that coffee. It's going to be a long night."

CHAPTER THIRTY-SEVEN

Friday night
10:30 PM

Gavriil ground his teeth. His targets couldn't have simply disappeared into thin air. But that's exactly what they seemed to have done.

The police chief had never driven by the Go-Now Market. He'd sat there for well over an hour, watching the road. Finally, an older woman knocked on his car window and asked if he was okay. He'd had no choice but to move on.

He'd driven a loop between the scientist's apartment and The Prairie Center but had seen no signs of any of his targets. Finally, he headed back to the abandoned barn to regroup.

He checked his phone again. No response to the new text.

Deep voices drifted up into the loft from the dark field below. He pocketed the phone and listened. Two, maybe three, men. Close. Too close.

He reached for his gun then lowered himself to his stomach. Slowly, silently, he inched across the floor to the shuttered hayloft door. He pressed his right eye to a slit in the door and raised the gun to the wood.

Two large uniformed officers—state troopers—were clomping through the field in their noisy boots waving heavy duty flashlights around. Wild arcs of light bounced through the night. One of the beams lit up their faces for a flash—round, youthful countenances with upturned noses and bright blue eyes. They could have been brothers. Maybe they were.

Despite their size and their military bearing, neither of them seemed particularly threatening. He relaxed his finger on the trigger and strained to hear their words.

"... pointless exercise. Chief Clark doesn't even have a picture of this Russian dude. How are we gonna know if we find him?"

"I guess we better hope he's wearing one of those fur hats."

They guffawed.

"Check the barn?"

"Only if it's unlocked. Duty sarge said we're not going to be hit with any property damages claims for doing a favor for some local PD."

The wall vibrated as a metal-toed boot connected with a wallboard outside.

"Who's gonna file a claim for this place? It's been empty since I was in high school. I used to bring Ashleigh out here ..." He trailed off, no doubt savoring a memory of his teenage trysts.

"Still. You don't want to end up in the doghouse with sarge."

Gavriil nodded approvingly at the level-headed advice. He hoped the other officer followed it. He'd hate to have the deaths of two troopers on his hands. Americans responded fiercely when law enforcement officers were gunned down. It would complicate things.

The door rattled below.

"How's it locked from the inside?"

"Who knows, dude. Maybe they barred it so kids couldn't use it as a makeout spot. But it's locked or stuck or whatever. Let's move on."

Gavriil was pleased he'd taken the precaution of jamming a rod he'd found in a pile of scrap metal under the barn door handle. It probably wouldn't withstand concerted effort from four determined boots. But it was never intended to. It was meant to slow down anyone who might try to enter.

He pivoted and put the door in his sights. The conversation outside continued.

"Maybe there's another way in around back."

"Mason, our shift's over in thirty minutes. Let's hit the next two on this road then head back to the barracks and clock out. It's Friday night, maybe Ashleigh'll be at the bar."

"Ashleigh's married to an accountant over in Elm and has a whole mess of babies. Ah, screw it. Okay, let's go. Suds and Buds has fifty-cent drafts until midnight."

Gavriil listened to them walk away. He remained quiet and motionless for a full ten minutes after he heard the distant sound of their car engine come to life.

Once he was convinced they'd really left, he propped himself up against the wall in the dark barn and thought through his next moves.

His current situation was sub-optimal. The police chief was closing in—she'd called in help from the state to find a Russian man. The federal agents and his targets had gone missing. He had to assume the doctor and the scientist were in protective custody. He needed to smoke them out.

CHAPTER THIRTY-EIGHT

11:15 PM

Hannah's announcement supercharged the atmosphere in the house. Clausen and Thurman shooed Bodhi and Chief Clark out of the living room and put Hannah through her paces on her involvement with Zhang San.

After that, Clausen put aside San's journal and worked with Thurman to craft a response for the NCSC to send back to Fyodorovych. IN the meantime, Chief Clark formally interviewed formal interview about the night the Russian tried to kill her.

Only Bodhi was still. He sat in the kitchen drinking a cup of tea at the breakfast bar.

Thurman walked into the room in search of a coffee refill. As he poured himself another cup, he said, "We drafted the text for the guys back at the office to push out to Fyodorovych's phone."

"What does it say?"

"There's no qualified help available. He needs to handle his problem alone, but he has the go-ahead to eliminate the HUMINT."

"Hannah."

Thurman sat down on the stool next to him. "We're going to protect her."

"I know."

"It's a helluva thing, her being an asset."

Bodhi nodded. "What's going to happen to her after this?"

Thurman took a sip of coffee. He twisted his mouth into a sideways frown. He seemed to be mentally composing an acceptable answer, one that wasn't truthful, but not classified. Finally, the agent nodded to himself.

"She's agreed to cooperate. When she finishes up with Chief Clark, I'll interview her about the specifics of what she did for San. She already gave us the broad strokes. San stole seeds from the fields and passed them to her to analyze. She confirmed whether they were Maize46 or another experimental line and then told him what they were and how to care for them."

"Why didn't she just give him the seeds?"

"Security at Supra Seed's too tight. It would have triggered alarms. Same reason the Chinese couldn't just hack into the software system. They had to do it the old-fashioned way, run an agent, recruit an asset—they used a manual code to pass notes, for Pete's sake."

"Hannah knows the code?" That would piss Clausen off to no end.

"No. San taught her a simple substitution cipher—she showed Elise. Hannah doesn't know enough Cantonese characters to read San's book, but she's sure it would include the information she passed him about the seeds."

Bodhi made a small sound. It could have meant anything. Even he wasn't sure what it did mean.

"Look, she's going to get fired, obviously. And she'll have to enter a guilty plea. But if she tells us everything, she'll get a light sentence. And if she helps us apprehend Fyodorovych, she might not even do any time."

Unbidden, Bodhi's thoughts turned to Feng. He'd committed a crime and would be punished. That seemed right. Hannah had committed what was arguably a worse crime—a matter of national security, according to Clausen and Thurman—yet she might escape punishment. He wasn't sure how he felt about all that. He put that issue to the side to examine during a more peaceful moment. The pressing concern now was Hannah's safety.

"You're going to use her as bait." It was a statement, not a question, but Thurman answered it.

"No, we're going to use both of you as bait."

Gavriil read the text message slowly. He shook his head. They'd taken the bait. The second message to Bishkek, just as the first, had included one of a handful of agreed-upon key words. In this case it was the phrase 'wet work.' He'd even used it twice to ensure the restauranteur wouldn't miss it, because Ivan was known for being distracted.

To establish that the message had been received by its intended recipient and that the answer wasn't being made under duress, the response should have included a reference to 'Aquaman.'

It was a primitive—yet effective—early-warning system. Either Ivan's territory had been taken over by a competitor, which happened from time to time on the black market just like anywhere else, or the pair of federal agents had access to the cell phone traffic. He judged the latter possibility to be the more likely.

Which meant the agents were NCSC. Which meant that the response was an attempt to set a trap.

He read it again:

Qualified help not available. Handle alone. Authorized to take out HUMINT.

They wanted to draw him out. But he wasn't interested in a game of cat and mouse unless he was the cat. He removed the battery and SIM card from the phone and stowed the device itself in the bottom of an old feed barrel. Then he turned his mind to his problem.

CHAPTER THIRTY-NINE

Just after midnight, Saturday morning

B ette's radio crackled. "Chief, we've got reports of gunfire out near Jason Durbin's place. His wife called it in. She said it sounds like it's coming from the abandoned barn at the Mitskys' old place."

Bette cursed under her breath. "I'm on my way."

She pulled on a pair of shoes and tied the laces tight. Then she holstered her weapon and put on a blue windbreaker.

"I won't be long. It's probably just somebody shooting at deer near their property." She looked around the room. "Don't go anywhere. Lock the deadbolts and the chains, front and back, and don't let me in unless I say the password."

"Asterope?" Bodhi asked.

She smiled. "Asterope."

"I'll come with you," Thurman offered. "Just in case." He drained his coffee and put the mug upside down in the sink.

She eyed him for a long moment. She was certain the call had nothing to do with international espionage. "It's deer season."

"It's after midnight."

"I didn't know the NCSC had an interest in some drunk homeowner violating the sunrise to sunset rule." Then she shook her head. "Whatever, come along if you want. Just stay out the way."

"You got it."

He handed his cell phone to Clausen. "Trade phones with me. Troy's team will call my number first if they get any hits on Fyodorovych's location."

They traded phones. Thurman followed Bette outside. Hannah hurried over to the door. Bette heard the deadbolt snick into place then the clang of the chain lock as soon as Thurman closed the door behind him.

After he'd finished shooting furiously at the side of the barn, Gavriil moved the rental car to a driveway about a tenth of a mile away from on the other side of the road. Then sat on the hood and waited.

After a while, he spotted the police chief's truck coming from the west and tracked its progress to the barn through the binoculars. Despite the darkness of night in the country, he could see clearly. Gavriil had no need for night vision accessories—his powerful binoculars were military-issue to work even in extreme low-light conditions.

She wasn't alone, but for his purposes, it didn't matter. He watched as she and the male NCSC agent exited the vehicle and drew their firearms. They circled the barn, shined their flashlights in the windows, and finally went inside.

He ignored the instinctive, territorial urge to protect what had been his space. He'd taken everything he needed with him. He wouldn't be returning.

The pair was inside for less than a minute. They came out and made a half-hearted search of the woods. When they emerged, he could see the police chief form the words 'like I said, probably just a drunk hunter.' The NCSC agent nodded.

He slid off the hood of the car and got behind the wheel. He waited until the police chief had started her engine. Then he started his.

He waffled for a moment over whether to use his headlights. It was nearly one o'clock in the morning. Traffic, always sparse out here, would be nonexistent at this hour. His lights would alert his targets to the presence of another car on the road. But driving without them in the dark was foolish. He turned them on and dropped back.

The policewoman turned in at the dead man's farm. No doubt, the widow had called in the gunfire. The porch light blazed on.

Gavriil pulled to the edge of the road and killed his lights and engine to wait. The farmer's death had been unfortunate. He shouldn't have been out in his field so late. The scientist had moved at the wrong moment and his shot missed its target. He shrugged to himself. These things happened.

The police officer and the agent stood on the farmhouse porch. The woman answered the door with a robe tied tight over her nightclothes.

He imagined their conversation. The police chief would say they checked out the shots, it's nothing to worry about. Murmur some condolences. Tell the woman to get some rest. The grieving widow would thank them, tell them good night.

The porch light went out. He checked his rearview mirror. No lights coming up from behind him. A moment later, he spotted the truck proceeding down the driveway at a decent clip.

He put the binoculars on the seat and turned the key in the ignition. The police chief's truck zipped off the driveway onto the road. Gavriil crept off the shoulder and crawled along behind it, keeping it in his sights. He'd learned his lesson last time.

He didn't lose visual contact until twenty minutes later when the truck turned right into a long, blacktop driveway. He pulled over and scrambled out of the car with the binoculars. The driveway led to a wide garage set off to the right of a brick house. The garage was big enough to hold three, maybe four, vehicles.

The chief's car idled for a moment. Then the garage door rolled up. He shifted his angle and he spotted a white sedan and a black sedan side by side in two stalls.

Gotcha.

She pulled into the third stall. The taillights went dark. The chief and the agent walked out of the garage. The chief clicked a button on her keys and the door rolled down. The pair hustled to cross the yard and disappeared around a corner. A moment later a light came on in the back of the house. He guessed it was the kitchen—the female agent or the doctor or the scientist had heard them returning and was unlocking the door.

Gavriil smiled. He returned to the car and pulled it behind a worn wooden farm stand, out of sight from the road and from the police chief's nearest neighbors. Then he killed the engine, set the alarm on his watch, and stretched out on the back seat for a ninety-minute nap.

Clausen demanded the password, Chief Clark gave it, and Hannah unlocked the door. The chief and Thurman hurried inside and Hannah locked the door behind them.

"Must have been a hunter," Thurman said in answer to Clausen's unasked question.

Chief Clark poured herself a glass of water. "Did you make any headway on the code?"

Clausen nodded. "Some. Hannah's been helpful with the specialized agricultural terms."

Bodhi was mildly surprised; Clausen's acknowledgment hadn't sounded even a bit grudging. Hannah ducked her head and hid a smile.

"Did Troy call?"

Clausen handed him his phone. "Yes. Like last time,

they couldn't triangulate his response. There aren't three towers close enough. And he went off the grid within minutes of us sending the response."

"He must be turning off the phone when he's not using it," Chief Clark mused.

The NCSC agents exchanged a meaningful look.

Then Clausen said, "They think he's going a step farther and removing the battery and maybe the SIM card."

"You can track the phone when it's turned off?" the chief asked.

"Some agencies can," Clausen non-answered.

Bodhi looked down at the outline of his mobile phone in his pocket. Chief Clark arched an eyebrow.

"Zhang told me never to carry my phone when I was going to the dead drop," Hannah offered. "That's why I couldn't call right away ... when the shooting happened," she finished in a small voice.

Bodhi narrowed his eyes. "Wait. Fyodorovych took a shot at you at the dead drop, right?"

"Yes."

"So he knows about it. How can you be sure he didn't plant misinformation there?" The question was for the NCSC agents, but Hannah answered.

"I think he may have," she said slowly. "The reason I was going to the drop was because Zhang had left a seed for me—well, I thought he had—but it wasn't one of ours. That had never happened before. I signaled for him to contact me, but he didn't. He was ... dead by then. I left a note in the dead drop, but it was still there when I went to check it. The seed was so odd. Do you think ...?"

"It's right out of the Russian playbook. *Dezinformat-siya*—disinformation—is classic Russian tradecraft. He removed the seed San left and replaced it with a dummy to confuse you, interfere with China's progress, and advance his own mission. He got the seed he needed. Then he killed San and got the book. The only thing left to do was to kill you," Clausen told her not unkindly. "Housekeeping."

"But Bodhi found San's journal, and Fyodorovych's bullet missed," Chief Clark interjected. "So now, his mission has expanded to include killing both of you and retrieving that book."

Bodhi's mouth went sour. Despite the fact that he worked with corpses for a living and followed a religion that stressed the impermanence of this life, the knowledge that someone else was planning his death for him was uncomfortable. Judging by Hannah's face, which was taut with sheer dread, she felt the same way.

Nobody spoke.

Then Bodhi cleared his throat. "So what exactly is the plan to get this guy?"

"It's a work in progress," Thurman told him.

"Fantastic."

"We should sleep," Clausen announced. "We'll be fresh in the morning, and maybe Troy's people will come through overnight. There's a team working round the clock."

She and Thurman said their goodnights and left the room. Bodhi looked at Chief Clark.

"There's no plan, is there?" he asked.

"Plans are highly overrated. You two really should hit the hay, though. Because plan or no plan, tomorrow's going to be a big day."

CHAPTER FORTY

Saturday morning, shortly before dawn

Gavriil considered the pre-dawn assault to be something of a cliché. But he recognized that it was a cliché for a reason: it was effective. Sleep-addled, or even sleeping, targets, low light, the element of surprise—these were measurable advantages. So he made the necessary preparations. Then he put his plan into motion.

Bette's cell phone rang at five thirty-eight. She groaned. Four-odd hours of beauty rest weren't quite enough. She reached for the phone and groaned again. Everything ached.

"Clark."

"We got a call. Two officers down."

She sat bolt upright, instantly awake.

"Ours?"

"No, chief. Uh ... I'm not sure whose they are, to tell you the truth. We called in a lot of favors last night, you know?"

She did. "What did the caller say, exactly, Kelly?"

"Let me read the transcript to you, chief. He said, quote there are two dead officers in the abandoned barn near the Durbin farm end quote. Isn't that where you got the call of shots fired last night?"

Bette's stomach lurched. "I'm on my way. Call the hospital and have them send a medic out, just in case."

She pulled on her clothes and splashed water on her face. She crept down the stairs and scribbled a note for the others. She tiptoed out onto the porch in her socks and then put on her shoes. She looked up at the lightening sky. Venus and Spica, Virgo's brightest star, winked down at her. She took a deep breath and whispered a prayer. Then she ran toward the garage.

One down, Gavriil thought as he watched her car careen down the driveway in reverse and then squeal out onto the road. She passed him doing eighty before flipping on her lights.

He returned the battery and SIM card to his cell phone and drummed his fingers on the barrel of his weapon while he waited for the device to power up. Then he tapped out a message to Kyrgyzstan, read it over, and hit send.

He drove as fast as he dared to the market where he'd purchased the phone. He lowered the car window and pitched the device into the bushes behind the store. He did not remove the battery or the SIM card.

He sped back to watch the police chief's house so he'd know when the message had been intercepted by the pointy-heads at the NCSC.

Bodhi was sitting lotus-style on the end of his bed, eyes closed, meditating. He heard Thurman's phone vibrating but didn't react. Then the sounds of Thurman stumbling around the room, pulling on his clothes, registered. But he put up a screen door in his mind and the distractions stayed out of his consciousness.

He was trying to work through his feelings about Hannah. His attraction to her. And his anger at her. He sat for a long time but came to no resolution. When he opened his eyes, Thurman was gone.

He heard water running through the pipes. Someone was showering. He'd have a cup of tea out on Chief Clark's porch and then shower and get ready to face his day. He went downstairs and found an empty kitchen and two notes—one under the sugar bowl near the coffee maker; the other on the kitchen table.

He sat at the breakfast bar and examined them both. The sugar bowl note was scrawled in pen in messy, feminine cursive writing. It read:

Got a call re: a local law enforcement issue. Will be back ASAP. Remember, Asterope.

~~BC

The note from the kitchen table was printed in pencil in miniscule, precise capital letters:

Fyodorovych texted Bishkek again. He's getting another new phone from a market in town as soon as it opens and will text from the new number. But he screwed up and left the battery in. We've traced him to the Go-Now Market. It doesn't open for another hour. We going to bring him in. Chief, don't let the civilians go outside for any reason.

~~Clausen

Bodhi placed the notes side by side on the breakfast bar. Then he walked to the kitchen door and turned the deadbolt and secured the chain. He checked the front door. On his way back to the kitchen, he ran into Hannah in the hallway. She'd wrapped a thick towel around her wet hair like a turban and was dressed casually in sweatpants and a loose-fitting, long-sleeved t-shirt.

"Good morning. I was just coming to see if the chief has a hair dryer I can borrow."

He looked at her pale, tired face for a beat. Then he said, "She went out."

"Ah, I was hoping to avoid having to ask my roommate if she has one. Have you seen her this morning?" Hannah's voice was light.

"She's not here either. It's just us."

"Oh." She lowered her eyes then said, "That's actually lucky. I want to talk to you ... about things."

His chest squeezed. "I want to talk to you, too, Hannah. But I don't think this is the time."

She blinked and looked up at him. "Why not?"

He felt his pulse hammering in his throat. "Because we're about to have a visitor."

Confusion clouded her eyes. "A visitor? Bodhi, it's ten after six in the morning."

The sound of glass being smashed came from the kitchen, followed by the tinkling noise of shards hitting the hardwood floor.

"What do we do?" she whispered. Her breath came fast, shallow.

"Take a deep breath. And then we'll run." He pointed to the front door.

She nodded then inhaled deeply. She exhaled.

He looked down. They were both barefoot. Her hair was wet. His cell phone was in his bedroom charging. She was empty handed and had no pockets, so she had no phone either. But there was nothing to be done about it.

"Go."

They sprinted toward the front door.

Gavriil waited in the conveniently positioned deer stand across the street from the police-woman's house. One good thing about the American Midwest was all the hunters. He was ideally situated to pick off his targets when they came running through the front door.

Which they would.

He'd seen them conferring in the hallway after he'd lured the federal agents to the market. They'd realized they were alone in the house. Then he'd chucked the rock through the window and had raced to the tree stand.

He figured he had another forty minutes before either the police chief or the NCSC agents came speeding back to the house from the sites of the false alarms. He supposed that was another good thing about rural Illinois—it took forever to get anywhere.

He checked his watch. Any second now.

The door opened and a man and a woman appeared on the porch. He raised his gun and fired.

CHAPTER FORTY-ONE

As Bodhi burst through the door, a long ago memory popped into his mind. Leo Connelly, a federal agent he knew from home, had been escorting Bodhi out of his own house, concerned that a killer might be lying in wait. Leo'd angled his body to create a smaller target.

It seemed like a good thing to do under the current circumstances. He turned back to tell Hannah to do it, too, but she wasn't there.

He looked down. She had rolled through the doorway and was crouching like a beast about to spring. The towel had come loose from her hair, which now cascaded wildly over her shoulders and face.

Ah, right, the kung fu black belt.

The first shot came and hit the doorframe, splintering the wood. Then the reporting boom sounded.

Hannah reached up and yanked his arm, pulling him to the porch floor. They sheltered behind the low brick knee wall that fronted the porch.

Brick was good, Bodhi thought. *But not bullet-proof.*

"What do we do?" Hannah hissed.

"Maybe we try to make it back inside. Coming out here was a mistake." He'd been so sure Gavriil had been on his way through the kitchen window.

From the field across the street, their assailant fired another shot. It hit one of the stepped brick walls that edged the stairs to the road below and lodged in the masonry.

"No. Out here we have more options. We'd be trapped in the house. Where is he?" Her pupils were dilated but her voice was steady.

"I think he's in the wooded lot across the way. He's shooting at us from under cover of the trees."

"There's probably a deer blind over there. Lots of folks have tree stands on their property."

Bodhi talked it through. "So here's what we know. He's likely elevated, which gives him a greater shooting area and a better angle—but only if we're below him. So, better to stay on the porch as long as we can—off the ground. He's using a high-caliber rifle; the bullets are hitting the house before we hear the gunshot. And he's a terrible shot."

Hannah gaped at him.

"Forensic pathology, remember? I need to understand trajectories, distances, all that stuff. Now let's talk about your expertise. Could you neutralize him with your bare hands?"

"A former Russian intelligence officer? I doubt it. I'm pretty good with weapons fighting—a staff, a sword, or nunchucks. But I've never used any of them in a, um, street fight. Also, I don't have a weapon—that's a limiting factor."

"Here's another limiting factor—I don't think I can kill him if I have to. Not even to save my own, or yours. I don't *know* that. But I won't know until put to the test. And if we end up in a situation where I am put to that test ... I wouldn't want you to rely on me." It had to be said, so he said it.

She blanched. "It's good to know."

They stopped whispering. Bodhi waited for the next shot to come.

Nothing.

They waited some more, crouched in the corner of the porch. The cool morning air was still and quiet. The sky was edged with pink. No cars or trucks drove along the road. No birds chattered. A typical rural morning—just add gun-toting Russian and stir, Bodhi thought.

"He's got to be on the move," Hannah said. "He would have taken another shot by now."

Bodhi twisted his neck to meet her eyes. "I have an idea. It might work."

"What's the worst case scenario if it doesn't?"

"Worst case is he kills us both. Most likely outcome is he kills me and you get away."

She leaned forward. "Wait. I have to tell you something—just in case. I let you believe that Zhang was my lover because I couldn't bear for you to know that I was helping him spy on Supra Seed. I didn't want you to think less of me." She lowered her eyes.

He didn't know how he would have responded given the chance. Just then another bullet tore through the air. This one whizzed just overhead and cracked Chief Clark's front window.

"He's getting closer. I have to do this now."

He kissed the top of her head. Then he crawled on his hands and knees to the corner of the wall. He stopped where the wall met the stairs. He took what he hoped was not his last deep breath. Exhaled. Then he stood and stepped into view at the top of the stairs, his hands pointed to the sky.

He took two steps down and stood on the stairs.

"You have a problem," he said in a clear voice to the

man who was advancing across the street with a gun pointed at his chest.

Gavriil's finger danced on the trigger. Then he blinked.

"What did you say?" He stopped in the middle of the road and waited for the doctor to respond.

"I said you have a problem. Actually, you have two."

Gavriil glanced down at his gun then laughed. "I think you're the one with the problem. I'm the one with the firearm."

The doctor nodded, hands still in the air. "You do have a gun. And I don't want to anger you, given that you're armed. But, I can't help noticing you're not a very good shot. I mean, assuming you were trying to hit us."

Red anger flared in Gavriil's belly. But it died instantly. It was objectively true. He was not the most accurate of marksmen from a distance. He never had been. And the silencer, which was a necessity, altered velocity and point of impact. Which, he believed, was why he hit the farmer and not the woman.

"I'm not great from a distance. I do okay at close range." He gestured with the gun for emphasis.

"That still doesn't solve your problems."

Gavriil eyed the doctor. The man was tense but resolved. There was no sign of the scientist. He assumed she was hiding on the porch. He considered shooting out one of the doctor's kneecaps. Just to make a point. But he decided to hear what he had to say. Then, he'd just shoot to kill. Gavriil wasn't a monster. He was a professional.

"Start talking."

"You need to kill us and get San's encrypted journal —right? The one I took from the trunk in the monks' basement."

At the reminder of the theft, Gavriil's rage returned. He tamped it down.

"That's right."

"But you also need to decrypt it. I mean, it's useless if it's encrypted."

"Also correct."

"So here's the problem. Ms. Lin is the only person who can decrypt it for you. So you need her alive."

Gavriil narrowed his eyes. "You're lying. Or deluded. My employer has a stable of decryption experts. And access to freelance talent. Cracking that code doesn't hinge on some random plant scientist."

"But it does. The NCSC has a stable of decryption experts, too. You know what the NCSC is, right?"

"Yeah, we're acquainted."

"The blonde agent, she's an expert in manual

decryption. And she can't crack it. Did you know there are more than fifty thousand written characters in Chinese? And San applied two ciphers. And he used both Cantonese and Mandarin. And, this is the crucial part, he and Ms. Lin decided on the universe of characters they'd use together. Even a computer algorithm can't break that code. Only Ms. Lin can."

Gavriil shook his head. "San wouldn't be that stupid. What if she got cold feet? What if I turned her? Or she got hit by a tractor? You can't be telling the truth."

The doctor shrugged. "I guess you could kill her and find out. But then your employer will probably be upset. If only two people know a code and you kill them both, the code dies with them. I mean, sure, maybe fifty years from now, some enterprising computer scientist will stumble on the solution. Assuming the population doesn't starve before then—or agree to be annexed by the United States in exchange for some food. You could get lucky."

Gavriil clenched his jaw. What if he was telling the truth? "What's the second problem?"

"Your second problem is that we don't have the book. It's in a hidden compartment in the trunk of the NCSC agents' car. That's easy enough to confirm. You can kill us both then search the house. Of course, then you'll have no journal, no one to decode the journal you don't have, and a whole list of felony charges. You might get away before the others come back and evade capture, but still, I imagine you'll be in trouble back at the office, as it were."

Gavriil was sorely tempted to shoot him just to shut him up.

Then the doctor glanced behind him to his right. When he looked back at Gavriil, his eyes were wide with surprise.

"I guess you actually have three problems."

"Oh, yeah?"

"Yeah. Ms. Lin seems to have vanished."

CHAPTER FORTY-TWO

For a while, Hannah huddled in the corner of the porch, trying to stop trembling, while Bodhi spun lie after lie for Fyodorovych. Once she'd gained some sort of control over her limbs, she started to think.

Bodhi's tactic would stall the Russian. Maybe for a good while.

But ultimately he'd find the book and then she'd be in trouble. If he didn't believe she was the only one with the code, he'd just execute her and Bodhi. If he *did* believe Bodhi's story, she foresaw an unpleasant episode of being tortured to break a code she actually couldn't break. She might survive that. The police chief and the NCSC agents had to come back sometime.

But what if he killed Bodhi, grabbed the book, snatched her, and took off? She'd be his prisoner.

She looked behind her. The porch wrapped around to the side of the house. Not all the way—but it extended about six feet back. She rolled to the edge. Then silently, like the ninja she'd grown up dreaming she'd become, she dropped to her feet in Chief Clark's flowerbed.

She could hear Bodhi talking on and on, and Fyodorovych's staccato expressions of disbelief. She hunched down and duckwalked toward the backyard, hewing tight to the wall.

She burst into a low run when she spotted Chief Clark's shed. She knew it would be locked. Of course it would be locked, the owner was the chief law enforcement officer for the county. But it would provide cover while she planned her next steps.

Because hope never dies she tried the shed door anyway. Locked.

She crept around to the back of the shed.

Standing in a plastic bucket was a fishing pole. Hannah pictured rods, tackle, and related fishing accessories in the shed. Lined up in tidy rows, neatly put away, until the chief's next fishing trip. But this rod was bent and broken. It was destined for the trash heap. A limp tangle of fishing wire hung from it.

Hannah smiled. She had to stop herself from laughing out loud and giving away her position.

Now, Fyodorovych really did have a problem. He just didn't know it yet.

The irate Russian wrenched Bodhi by the arm and dragged him through the open front door in search of Hannah. Bodhi considered pointing out that Fyodorovych would have seen Hannah if she'd slipped through the door while they were talking. But, he estimated that there were better than even odds that the spy would shoot him if he did. So he held his tongue.

He was glad he had no clue where Hannah had gone. There was no chance he'd give away her hiding spot, either inadvertently or as the result of being tortured. He was reasonably sure Fyodorovych was going to kill him sooner or later. At least he would die knowing that Hannah had escaped into the woods behind the chief's house and would get to safety.

"Where is she?" Fyodorovych growled.

"I don't know."

He shoved Bodhi forward toward the kitchen, scanning each room they passed for signs of movement. Bodhi could feel the man's anxiety ratcheting up. Fyodorovych was racing a ticking clock. Soon, Chief

Clark and NCSC would return. And then Fyodorovych would be outgunned.

Through the window over the kitchen sink, Bodhi spied a flash of black. Hannah's dark hair. It streamed behind her as she weaved through the trees at the edge of the lawn.

He glanced at Fyodorovych. He gave no sign of having seen her. He was busy reading the notes from Chief Clark and Clausen. He gave a satisfied grunt.

"Sit." He pulled out the chair closest to him and pushed Bodhi into it.

Bodhi maintained a neutral expression. Fyodorovych had placed him facing the front door.

"I'm going to have a look around. If you move, I'll shoot you in the leg. If you yell, I'll shoot you in the mouth. Any questions?"

"No."

Bodhi tracked Fyodorovych's progress around the kitchen as he opened drawers, turned over baskets, and pawed through the freezer in an apparent effort to find San's journal. Out of the corner of his eye, Bodhi also watched as Hannah padded barefoot through the front door. She held a length of fishing wire, each end of which was tied to a stick. An improvised garrote.

She tilted her head to the side. *Where is he?*

Bodhi twitched his own head slightly to his right,

toward the refrigerator, in a quick motion then yanked it back.

She nodded and pressed herself against the wall. She slinked toward the kitchen. He averted his eyes, afraid to give away her position, and returned his attention to the Russian, who was now rifling through a stack of cookbooks.

Bodhi risked a glance. Hannah had reached the corner where the hallway and the kitchen intersected. She held the garrote in front of her, ready.

Fyodorovych had shoved the gun in his waistband to conduct his search. Even if he pulled it, there'd be a delay. Bodhi pushed off from the edge of the table and tipped the heavy oak chair back on two legs. As he headed for the floor, he imagined every muscle in his body relaxing, growing heavy and limp. The chair crashed to the ground.

"What the—" Fyodorovych turned and stalked angrily toward Bodhi. He pulled his gun out and aimed it at the toppled over chair as he approached. "Stay there."

As the man crossed the hallway, Hannah reached out like a shadow and looped the fishing line around his neck from behind. She pulled the sticks, stretching the wire tight across his neck. The wire applied pressure to

Fyodorovych's carotid arteries and respiratory tract. He slipped out of consciousness within seconds.

Bodhi took cover under the table in case the gun fired when it hit the floor. But it bounced out of Fyodorovych's hand and landed, inert, as its owner collapsed facedown in a heap. Bodhi ran to Hannah, who was staring down at the Russian with a horrified silent scream etched on her face.

"Did I ... is he dead?"

Bodhi gently moved her to the side. "No. He's unconscious. You cut off the supply of oxygen to his brain. He might wake up stupider, but who'd be able to tell? He will wake up though—pretty quickly. We have to hurry. Get the gun."

She nodded and ran to retrieve the weapon. He removed the fishing line from Fyodorovych's neck and looped it around the man's wrists, pulling his hands together near his tailbone. He tied a quick surgeon's knot and pulled it tight. Then he used his foot to nudged Fyodorovych onto his side. The Russian was already moaning.

Hannah pointed the gun down at him. "Be quiet."

She gave Bodhi a sidelong look. "Now what?"

"Now we wait for the cavalry."

CHAPTER FORTY-THREE

Sunday morning, before sunrise

Bodhi and Bette sat on her back porch and gazed up at the morning star, bright in the gray pre-dawn. She pointed out other stars and planets, rattling off names between sips of coffee. Bodhi listened and drank his tea.

When the shining Pleiades constellation at last faded into the background and the sun streaked pink and orange across the horizon, Bette said, "Thurman texted me. The NCSC is finished interviewing Hannah. She'll be back from Chicago tonight—are you sure you don't want to stick around another day?"

"I'm sure."

A moment passed.

"She's been very cooperative, according to Thurman."

"I'm glad."

"Fyodorovych isn't talking. But it really doesn't matter. They have what they need."

Bodhi nodded. "All in all, things worked out as well as they could have."

That drew a snort of laughter. "I have a monk in jail, a dead farmer, a dead Chinese spy, and a farmer who lost a field to arson. It hasn't been a banner week for Onatah."

He smiled. "But I met you."

Her eyes sparked. "Me?"

"You know what's curious about the Pleiades, Bette? Alcyone draws all the attention because she shines so bright, but it's elusive Asterope that's the double star. I thought Hannah was vulnerable and needed rescuing. Turns out, she rescued herself. I'm genuinely happy things are going to turn out okay for her. But she also got herself into her mess because she wasn't steady. Asterope is steady. And bright. That's my kind of star."

He felt enormously stupid and lapsed into silence.

Bette placed her mug on the deck railing and leaned over. Her silvery hair made such a contrast with her quick green eyes and her smooth face. For an instant she looked like an elf, not a badass police chief.

She pressed her lips against his in a warm, firm kiss. He tasted coffee. He took her face in his hands. After a long moment, she pulled back and searched his face.

"Are you sure you want a ride to the bus depot this morning?" Her breath was hot on his cheeks.

He swallowed. "On second thought, what's one more day?"

THANK YOU!

Bodhi will be back in his next adventure soon! If you enjoyed this book, I'd love it if you'd help introduce others to the series.

Share it. Please lend your copy to a friend.

Review it. Consider posting a short review to help other readers decide whether they might enjoy it.

Connect with me. Stop by my Facebook page for book updates, cover reveals, pithy quotes about coffee, and general time-wasting.

Sign up. To be the first to know when I have a new release, sign up for my email newsletter at www.melissafmiller.com. I only send emails when I have book news —I promise.

While I'm busy writing the next book, if you haven't read my Sasha McCandless, Aroostine Higgins, or We Sisters Three series, you might want to give them a try.

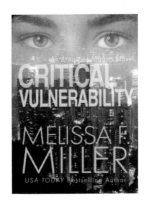

ABOUT THE AUTHOR

USA Today bestselling author Melissa F. Miller was born in Pittsburgh, Pennsylvania. Although life and love led her to Philadelphia, Baltimore, Washington, D.C., and, ultimately, South Central Pennsylvania, she secretly still considers Pittsburgh home.

In college, she majored in English literature with concentrations in creative writing poetry and medieval literature and was STUNNED, upon graduation, to learn that there's not exactly a job market for such a degree. After working as an editor for several years, she returned to school to earn a law degree. She was that annoying girl who loved class and always raised her hand. She practiced law for fifteen years, including a stint as a clerk for a federal judge, nearly a decade as an attorney at major international law firms, and several years running a two-person law firm with her lawyer husband.

Now, powered by coffee, she writes legal thrillers and homeschools her three children. When she's not writing, and sometimes when she is, Melissa travels around the country in an RV with her husband, her kids, and her cat.

Connect with me:
www.melissafmiller.com

ACKNOWLEDGMENTS

Many thanks to everyone involved in the production of this book—in particular, my phenomenal editing and design team.

Made in United States
North Haven, CT
14 February 2022

16125932R00181